Book 2
The Undercity Series

by Kris Moger

This book is dedicated to my mother because she's wonderful.

Like little extras?

Sign up for our newsletter at krismoger.com and get a FREE copy of Mischief and Magic, a collection of short stories and Undercity extras.

Chapter 1

Caden pressed her forehead and hands against the glass and stared out at a world she longed to experience. Green, the word thrived in her brain now. When she closed her eyes at bedtime, she imagined dripping leaves and swaying grasses. All night, she walked among the foliage—touching petals, holding flowers, imagining the feel of the breeze on her skin and the perfume of life in her nose. In the morning, she almost breathed scented air when she woke.

She flattened her palms against the windowpane, part of her wishing the glass would melt and let her out. But tempered panels such as this didn't break easy, according to her brother. Amid the wild greenery outside, crumbled, broken structures poked through like markers of times past. Why some people built their buildings to withstand the disaster and others didn't, she didn't understand.

Teddy insisted almost a full month passed since their ragged community settled in the tower. She paid little attention to how many days came and went; she just appreciated one more. The transition between their old existence and their new life shocked, in both good and bad ways, the hundred or so people who survived the trip. Life was good; people had water, air, food, and supplies in abundance here. And they had room, lots of room, enough for everyone to use a real bed, to be clean, and to live. Most people adjusted well to the new standard of living though some discovered new levels of greed and lust for more. For others, they hid, cowering and scrounging in the more dilapidated areas as though this was the life they understood and they would face nothing better.

Absently, she removed her headscarf and worked at the twists of her coarse hair, rubbing in the hair oil Pa scrounged up for her. Caden didn't understand. Who thinks of a pleasant room and a comfortable bed as anything evil? She blinked, eyes dry, and continued to stare at the fields and forest below. If they couldn't handle this, how would they ever survive going outside? Her breath caught at the idea. Outside—what a dream. It looked safe, but was it?

"Ma's been looking for you," said an ever-cheerful voice behind her.

She turned and smiled at Deb who sprawled out over her bed on her side of the room. Caden plopped down on her own bed near the window. At first, she didn't want to share a room with her little sister, but after a couple of nights of total silence, she found she couldn't sleep without Deb's mumbling in her sleep.

"I thought you were in Teddy's school. Bored so soon?"

Her sister scrunched her button nose and twirled a strand of blonde hair. They were so different, and not only because Caden was adopted. Deb exuded health and energy with sparkling blue eyes and an eternal smile while her own sable complexion was patchy and scarred. Vitality left her as though she had holes in the bottom of her feet that let everything out. She did not begrudge her little sister any though; she adored Deb like she was her own, having been with her since she was born. The little girl seemed to understand that no matter how gruff she was she didn't mean to be cranky with anyone. It was a security valve, a safe place to breathe. Any sense of caring terrified her like a long climb up a dilapidated staircase.

Deb went to the window, curling up on the ledge, a mysterious smile on her face. "No. School ended early today. Teddy is still trying to sort out the classes and stuff. He hasn't got enough books, 'n pencils, 'n other things he says he needs. The other kids all went to help out in the sunshine room."

"And you didn't want to go?"

"Nope."

Caden crawled off the bed and tugged on a grey sweater over her burgundy t-shirt. After, she pulled on the boots Pa scrounged for her and tucked her baggy grey pant legs into the tops. "Coming?" she asked as she went to the door.

Her sister shook her head. "Gonna go over to the playroom later."

"Have fun," she said and left the room and went into the hall which was gloomy despite the smattering of lights that worked. The one thing they did not find many of was light bulbs, particularly the long tube type that seemed to break easily.

As she loped through the passage, she ran her fingers along the wood trim halfway up the wall. Green paper puckered on the walls and peeled away in spots as though tired of holding on. The frantic pattern of the orange and brown rug, did little to ease her spirits. A spasm of pain coursed through the middle of her back and up her neck. The tendons in her hands resisted as she flexed them. Little gave way as she massaged her left shoulder, the muscles tight and fingers somewhat numb.

"Ma got a job for you too?" asked Jolon as he met her at the stairs. His soft curls of black hair shorn tight to his head, making his tawny face seem rounder than ever with his pudgy cheeks and lips. He made up the second youngest in their mismatched family and lived with them for over four years; yet still had not grown an inch upward though he expanded sideways.

Caden patted his head. "Yeah, baldy, nifty cut. You do that to yourself or get cornered by Mrs. Fish and her wayward scissors?"

Jolon stuck out his tongue, his cheeks flushing like apples. "Took a wrong turn and ran into her studying me like I was her next experiment. Would a run, but Pa showed up and thought a trim was a super idea. Trim, right, more like a shearing."

She chuckled as they headed down to the main floor and the table room where her mother made her headquarters. "On the shinier side, now you have less to wash."

"Ha, ha, funny," he huffed and straightened his shirt, tucking the plaid material in his dark pants. "Since we got to this place Ma caught some kinda clean bug. My teeth aren't even safe anymore since they found those little brushes."

They entered the plaza where the massive fountain with the sparkling lights stood. A few people lingered by the entrance to the darker part of the complex, but otherwise the place was quiet. The new settlement was a maze of interconnected tunnels and buildings with many areas yet to be explored. Caden preferred to keep to the familiar areas, scrounging no longer holding her interest.

"Yeah, they took all my favourite clothes away the other day. Even my purple sweater right when it reached the right level of comfort and wear."

"Meh, I hid mine," her brother said, his hands jammed in his pockets and forehead wrinkled. "No one is gettin' anything more from me that I don't want to give up."

Caden grinned at him and spied a familiar figure by the fountain. "Hey, there's Cate," she said, waving to the girl sitting on the fountain's ledge, her arm in the water. Her coils of rusty hair almost touched the rippled surface of the pool as she strained to get whatever held her attention. Grime streaked her face and stained her ragged shirt while a long brown belt cinched her baggy grey pants to her waist.

"You're gonna fall in if you bend over anymore," Caden said as they came up beside her. She smiled at her long-time friend who came from the same dark place in Undercity she grew up in. Unlike Caden who, despite her hunched shoulders, was tall and never kept on any weight. Her friend was solid in build, like she hoarded muscles in case of a shortage. Short and stalky described her best, but she had an engaging smile when coaxed out of her. Other differences went deeper than physical. Both had weaknesses which left them scrambling to survive. Cate trusted no one or anything enough to be comfortable in a community. Fierce in her independence, she stayed in the darker part of the mall with the other hiders, so finding her out in the center of everything surprised Caden.

She nudged Cate on the leg. "Here, let me help. My long arms gotta be useful sometimes."

The other girl screwed up her face in a frown, but sat up, shaking her dripping arm. Her hair covered half her face and hid her empty eye socket from sight.

"Fine. Get the marble in that corner." She gestured to a large blue stone under the surface.

"That piece of glass, what do you want that for?" Jolon asked in his usual forthright manner.

Cate glared at him with her one grey-blue eye. "That's none of your business."

Jolon shrugged as though he didn't care. "Wonderful to see moving hasn't changed everything," he grumbled as he glared back. "Meet you at the kitchens, Caden." He shuffled off in his plodding way.

"You could get along with him," Caden suggested as she knelt over the fountain and reached for the stone.

"You get along with him. I think he's a blob," her friend retorted as she waited, her teeth working over her bottom lip. She picked up a teacup filled with candle wax resting on the edge of the fountain and stared at the tiny flame flickered in the center.

"Pretty. Where'd you find that?" Caden asked, nodding toward the candle.

Cate ran a finger around the rim. "Made it. Found a bunch of broken candles and some cups. Thought they'd work well together, so I melted the wax and there you go."

Caden grinned. "Clever."

"Beats stumbling in the dark," she said with a shrug and a small smile.

"Yeah, don't miss that," Caden said, remembering the times when they huddled together in the dirt and darkness, making cutting remarks about everything around them. Every morning they would wake up to gnawing hunger and shivering cold. The rest of the time they scrounged for scraps and hid in the shadows to avoid unwanted attention.

When Caden's adoptive parents took her in, they offered to help Cate too, but she didn't trust anyone. Even though the years proved their hearts and actions true, it was as if Cate thought happiness was impossible for her. She visited Caden, but avoided the rest of the family.

Caden captured the glass ball in her fingers, her right hand joints complaining against the cold. "Here you are," she said with a smile, and held the little orb up. "Nice."

Cate took the stone and clutched it in close as though she thought someone would snag the treasure from her. "Yeah, found it in a shop. Thought the size was about right..." she stopped, clamping her lips shut and avoiding Caden's gaze.

"Good scrounge," Caden said, knowing better than to press. As she got up and put a hand through her hair. "Well, I gotta go, but we could get together later?" She tried not to make her words sound like a plea, but she missed her friend like she would miss half of herself.

The other girl made a derisive gesture as she got up. "I'm sure you'll have other things to do."

Caden caught her arm. "I won't. And if I do, you can join me."

"What and obey?" she mocked with a hollow laugh. "Sure, I can mince along like you."

The words took her off guard. She released her hold and Cate hurried away. Her friend disappeared into the shadows of the undeveloped part of the mall. A heavy sigh escaped from Caden's lips as she rose and straightened her stiff back. Confused, she pushed all thoughts of Cate aside before shuffling toward the kitchen. Instinctively, she hunched and cast her eyes downward upon entering the table room, her usual stance when confronted by a room full of people. The space was huge with only a few survivors around, but they still scared her. Teddy sat at a table with several girls and guys around their age. Since the move, her brother had become popular. Many painted him and Pa as heroes, which irked like a pinprick in the side. Somehow tower residents forgot her part as though she wasn't present when they discovered a way to paradise.

"Hey," Teddy called as he sauntered over. Several of those vying for his attention rolled their eyes at her, but he showed no interest in them. He changed a little in the last couple of months. His clothes were tidy and his smile ever ready, but he still had circles under his eyes from late nights with books and writing. His chestnut hair still hung in a mess. However, he appeared older now, taller and more square, his khaki tinted face more angular.

"Hey, yourself," she answered back with a grimace and a nod to the crowd behind them. "Your fandom is growing."

"My what?" He glanced behind him. "Oh, ahh, they're searching for something to do. It's funny, before we kept busy surviving and now pickings are so easy everyone seems lost." He nodded toward her, his hands stuffed in his pocket and shoulders slouched.

She never realized he and Jolon had the same habit before. Which one picked the quirk up from the other, she couldn't guess.

"You going to visit Ma?" he continued as he fell in step with her.

"Yep. She probably has some weird new recipe for me to try out."

They left via a swinging door and went along a walkway with a cement floor and dirty walls. Tables and carts lined one side, narrowing the aisle. The path turned left at the end and opened to a noisy kitchen of shouting cooks and their drudges. Pots and pans banged and swung about while knives flicked over root vegetables. Overhead, lights flickered from power fluctuations. Mrs. Fish waved at them from her station by the stove and they nodded at a few more people while making their way to the back room where their mother worked.

"Close the door," Ma ordered as they came in. She sat at a desk covered in papers and books; her wild pale hair tied in a neat bun and her boney face, flushed. Her narrow fingers flipped through pages as though she searched for the answers to life's problems.

"What to do, what to do," she muttered. She slammed shut the book in her hands and shook her head at them. "I am amazed at the variety of food people made in the past, so many meals. Stretches the imagination to think of them. Pasta, stews, salad, the variety of ingredients alone is staggering." A smile spread over her face. She was lord of her domain, creating meals out of whatever she could cook.

"Something interesting for supper tonight, Ma?" her brother asked.

"Doubtful," she said with a sigh. "But it'll still be good." She reclined in her chair and put her feet up on her desk, stretching her arms behind her. The folds of her long skirt fell back and revealed her knee-length, black socks and worn runners. "Tired," she yawned. "Need to start a cooking rotation, train some of the others to take over. Then I could take one of those long soaks I keep hearing about without anyone running in on me 'cause the soup's burning."

"Isn't Nuna helping?" Teddy asked.

Ma shrugged at the mention of the original inhabitant of the towers. "The sudden influx of all these people has overwhelmed her somewhat. She doesn't come around too often. Nuna informed me in our last conversation that it was the Peterson family," she waved a hand at all of them, "who wanted to help everyone, so it was the Peterson family who could sort out all the details. Not so nice, I know, but I think she'll come around once everything settles. She had been alone for quite a long time."

Caden played with a little statue of a duck on her mother's desk. "Deb said you wanted me for something."

"Yes, Henri is watching the tunnel and he must be hungry by now. You and your brothers go bring him that box of food." She gestured to a cardboard box by the door.

"The load's not so big, Ma, I don't think this task will take three of us," Caden objected, sensing an ulterior motive.

Their brute brought her flowers every day when they lived in the warehouse. When they moved, he started bringing her everything he thought she might want from different stores. At first, his attention annoyed and frightened her. No one had ever been sweet on her before and she doubted anyone ever would again. Then she found it wonderful for the same reasons. Now, she was miffed and tired because he did nothing else. He didn't like to talk much, or read, or even hold hands. He gave her things and mooned over her from afar. So she avoided him even though her mother thought they made a wonderful match and liked to promote the idea whenever possible.

Her mother wagged a digit her way and held out a list. "Go with your brothers and gather these ingredients. They're mostly spices and dried teas. Your pa said to check a couple of the stores listed."

Teddy took the list from her. "Sure, Ma. Will do."

Caden remained silent, but her mother narrowed her gaze and gave her a slight nod and a grin. Caden got the message. Sighing, she left with Teddy who took the crate on his way out. Jolon was leaning against one counter, munching on slices of raw potato.

"To the mall, mates," he said with a potato salute.

"To the mall," Teddy agreed with a jaunty grin.

Caden tried to match their relaxed camaraderie, but found her wary nature blocking her way. A hollow ache, worse than hunger, sat in her stomach. Yes, life was better now, but she longed for more.

Teddy put the food on a small cart and pulled it behind him as they left. "Let's go the back way through the halls and out into the lobby."

Jolon chuckled. "Tired of your fans?"

"He's afraid they'll follow us in a parade with banners and such," Caden added, winking at Jolon.

"Funny, so funny," Teddy retorted. "It's faster, that's all."

They both nodded in false agreement, grinning at him. He ignored them and kept going. Their cart rattled across the grey and blue tiles as they went. They passed the central desk and climbed the steps leading to Henri. People milled about, sifting through the ransacked shops.

"There's not too much left that's useful on this level," Teddy told them as they went by store after store. Soon, the place emptied until they were among the few people left.

A person or two made their home in some of the stalls, draping the entrances and windows with strips of cloth and blankets. The dull glow of meagre flickering lights lit their way. Most of the lights no longer worked, and those that did were lengths apart.

It took a while to get back to the area where they first discovered their new home. When they arrived, they found Henri pouring over a book. He looked up as they approached, his massive posture embarrassed as he tucked the book behind his back.

"Oh, uh, hi," he muttered with an odd wave. The move did not change him at all. He was still lumpy muscular with thin brown hair and a hopeful grin on his ash face. He didn't stink so much though.

"Hey," she responded with a shy nod. The expectation of a romantic relationship was irritating. Why couldn't they be friends?

Jolon sat on a bin next to him. "You taken up reading?" He grunted as Teddy ran the cart into him. "Hey, careful."

"He's trying to tell you it's supposed to be a secret," Caden whispered to Jolon and shook her head. "Why hide it, Henri?"

He twitched a bashful shrug. "Dunno."

The brute took on such an uncomfortable expression she let the matter go. "Well, we've brought you some food. Ma sent enough for a dozen people, so this should last you for a few hours. How long are you posted here?"

He shrugged again and took the box. "'Till night." A stiff grin spread across his face. "Thanks."

This time she shrugged. "Gotta feed ya. Who would protect us otherwise?"

Henri chuckled and took something from behind his back. "For you."

Caden took the shiny black kitty figurine and tried to smile back. "Thanks."

Teddy leaned against one of the cement boulders blocking the access to their new home. "Any action?"

"Nope," Henri answered as he sunk his teeth into a potatocake.

"Doubt there would be." Jolon stuffed a cushion under his backside. "Even if they managed to cross the bridge, it would be a miracle if they found this place after we hid the entrance so well."

"Do you honestly think any of them would bother?" she asked.

"Bother what?" Teddy asked.

She found a plastic crate to sit on and rested her legs. The walk caused the ache to come back, so she rubbed them. "Bother trying to get to us. I mean, what's the point? Now, there are less of them to provide for, but they still have enough Underlings to dig for them. Why bother seeking what is gone?"

"I figure they think we're all dead," Jolon added.

Teddy frowned. "Georges doesn't think so. She figures they believe we found something better than what they possess, and they want it. She says they probably met with each other and talked themselves into a frenzy of selfishness and revenge, so we should keep a vigilant eye on everywhere."

Georges, Caden sniffed at the mention of the strange Upperlord with the cynical intelligence and apathetic demeanour.

"They removed her title."

Caden arched an eyebrow at Teddy. "Why? What does a title matter here?"

Her brother shrugged. "Dorkas threw a fit and got everyone riled up."

"He's good at that."

"Yeah, well, he convinced the other elders that as long as Georges held a title she would always be above everyone; therefore, everyone else would always defer to her."

She laughed at this. "Yes, because that's what Dorkas wants. While Georges holds such a distinction, Dorkas can't."

"That's ridiculous, true, but ridiculous." Jolon brushed dirt from his trousers, his expression one of bored annoyance.

"Why want title? Just words." said Henri who finished eating half his food and put the rest away on a corner table near his chair.

"It's not just the words," Teddy explained. "It's the power that goes with them. Now that Dorkas discovered all this place offers, he wants more."

"Jolon right, that red... redicu... ridiculous."

"Especially since our community consists of only, what, a couple hundred of us?" said Caden. She stretched her arms above her head as her back seized. "What's the point of lording over anyone?"

"Some people like power," Teddy said and Caden guessed by his blank face his mind flitted back to the stories he read.

The discovery of the shops led to a whole new world of resources for Teddy's insatiable appetite for reading and knowledge. Though Caden never enjoyed reading—the lines always seemed to get away from her—she did love to listen. Often, in the evenings, he would read to her and the others stories from his new books or something he scratched out himself. It was a good ritual. She liked rituals. They made her feel safe, consistent within such boundaries. The greatest difficulty she found adjusting to their new home was the departure from everything familiar. Though all their rooms were clustered together, they no longer had a common space for only their family. Nor did they catch each other as they were going by. Now the doors were always closed and she had to knock to gain access. Not that that was too hard, but it seemed more intrusive—separated and distant. They ate at the same table, but in a horde of people. They gathered in the common area and others joined them. It was both crowded and lonely.

"We should head back," Teddy decided as he stood.

"Yeah," Jolon said with a dramatic weary stretch as though hard labour awaited him.

"Go now?" Henri asked, his open face tragic. He got up and gazed at Caden with hopeful puppy eyes.

She managed an awkward smile and rose to her feet. "We'll talk to you later, Henri. Ma always has stuff for us to do and Deb wanders off."

He slumped in the shoulders and nodded. "K."

They left him and headed back in silence for most of the way. Everyone wanted her to like Henri and she did, but not like Ma liked Pa and vice versa. Love and intimacy like that confused and scared her.

Chapter 2

"You two want to help me re-organize the school?" Teddy asked as they entered the lobby and sat down on one of the long couches by the fountain.

Jolon stretched his short legs out and put his hands behind his head. "I'm not a reader."

"Well, you don't need to be," Teddy told him. "You like to figure things out, make things. I got an idea that we could create a kind of science and mechanics section. Hanna might help and Pa too."

He scratched his head as though checking to see if the thought sunk in. "Sounds not too bad. I like stuff."

Teddy grinned and turned toward Caden, who stared back, wondering what he expected her to say. She didn't like reading or messing with mechanical stuff, so what did he expect her to do?

"What?"

"I want your help."

Suspicious, she narrowed her gaze. "Why?"

"Because," he said and chuckled.

"Oh, clever. Terrible reason. Give up, brainy. What's going on under that head of hair?"

"You're artistic and I'm not."

She agreed. Books, numbers, and such came easily to him, but he couldn't draw worth anything.

"Plus, you're clever with the little ones."

"Ah, no." She put her hands up in protest, shaking her head. "I'm not babysitting. I'm good with Deb 'cause she's my sister. The rest are drownable."

Jolon laughed. "Ha, she took care of Mrs. Fish's five last week and tied 'em up together and told them the game was capture. They were captured, and their job was to stay that way. Funny thing, they had fun."

"Okay, so not so good with the little kids." Teddy chuckled but hid it in a cough. "You are good at art, though."

Before she answered, Ma and Mrs. Fish came hurrying up. "Good, you're back," their mother said, out of breath.

"What's up, Ma?" Jolon asked, "You lose a potato?"

She cuffed him on the side of the head. "Don't be impertinent. Deb's missing."

The three of them jumped to their feet at this.

Teddy assumed Pa's authoritative stance of hands on hips and feet spread wide. "What do you mean, missing?"

"She was playing with my two youngest and they said she took off. Apparently, she wanted to be an explorer like her Pa and left down one of the tunnels," Mrs. Fish said, her hand on their mother's back and her broad golden face serious. "Don't worry, dear, I'm sure she didn't go far. We'll get a search and get her back."

"We'll go, Ma," Caden inclined her head toward her brothers. "We know these tunnels best of everyone. We also know Deb. We'll bring her back."

The boys agreed with her, and their mother put a hand to her chest.

"Yes, and you tell that daughter of mine she'll not get any supper tonight for scaring me to death."

"They were making up games in the northern halls," Mrs. Fish told them. "Lower floor by the chicken side of the gardens. They weren't supposed to go anywhere else. They knew better."

"Yes, but she's her father's daughter," Ma said, her lips thin.

As they left, she collapsed on the couch, her face pale. Mrs. Fish sat beside her, holding her hand and whispering soothing words.

"We better grab our gear," Teddy said with a hint of enthusiasm in his voice.

"Oh, fun. Here we go again, digging through garbage," Jolon muttered though he lacked conviction in his complaint.

Both of them hurried about with more energy than usual. She too felt a rush of adrenaline. None of them went scrounging since they settled here. No one had a reason. The stalls and tower contained, so many supplies no one needed to scrounge anymore. Hanna discovered all that seemed useful. They found paradise, what else did they need to search for?

Yet, they forgot scrounging gave them a purpose and hope. They always had somewhere to go and something to discover.

"Deb is fine," said Teddy as though feeling a tinge of guilt over his enthusiasm. "I figure she went down one of the halls and got scared, so she hunkered down."

"Yep, right," said Jolon as they went into the storage room where they stored the scrounging equipment. "The tanks still good on air?"

Caden checked the gauges. "Pretty much. Got enough for a couple of hours. We should bring an extra for Deb." She slung her stash over her shoulder and snatched up a light. "Water, we need water."

Teddy stuffed a stash with a shovel, a light, a pry bar, and another tank. "Jolon, run back to the kitchen and get some snacks. We'll meet you in the sunroom."

"Run, right, me? Sure, you're expecting lots," Jolon retorted, but he left anyway.

"You up for this?"

Caden tightened the straps to her pack. "Always. Keep up, all right?"

His grin fluctuated between excitement and concern. "I shouldn't be this excited. Deb could be in real trouble."

She squeezed his arm. "Yeah, but I missed this too. Funny how scrounging gets in the core and makes a home."

With a heave of his shoulders, he inhaled to his toes as though preparing for battle. "Yep, you cut me, and I bleed junk."

They hurried to the sunshine room. Caden blinked as her eyes adjusted to the rays of light flowing in from the windows overhead. Many people gathered in the brightness and managed the gardens created in the rows of large planters that surrounded the area. The sweet scent of blossoms tinted the moist air. As beautiful as the place was, it always made her uncomfortable.

The first night they arrived from their old home, Teddy took them all down to check out the stars that twinkled so high up. The vastness of space and the idea that more than the walls surrounded her—overwhelmed her. She watched the rain with them once, but other than that, she avoided the room.

Jolon joined them a few moments later, and the three of them set off. They left the sunlight behind and went into the less explored areas of their new home. The halls were in rough shape compared to the rest of the place. Wallpaper hung in strips where water damage leaked through extensive cracks in the cement underneath. Dead lights and wires dangled from the ceiling and junk made the floor an obstacle run.

Smudges in the dirt—Caden shifted her eyes to Teddy. He bobbed his head in agreement, and they went on, following Deb's trail. She had skipped her way through the boxes and piles of junk, heedless of the possibility of danger before her.

"She was moving pretty recklessly," Jolon said.

"Yep," Caden replied, frowning. "You would think she would know better."

Teddy halted and took out his handlight as the passage got darker. "Why? Pa never took her out. She's never been anywhere but the warehouse."

Jolon pulled out a light too and flicked it on. "In all this freedom, I guess the temptation was too much."

"Careless child," Caden muttered. "Such an infuriating, careless kid. She has no air, no light, no nothing. I doubt she has any idea where she's going."

Her brother put a hand on her shoulder. "We'll find her."

"Not standing here," she said and shook him off. This wasn't the time for comfort. They had to hurry. Shoving stuff aside, they continued until they reached a pair of doors at the end of the hall.

Jolon came up behind her. "They are too heavy for her to open."

Teddy pushed on one door. It swung wide as though made of paper. "Closer's busted. Doesn't hold anything shut anymore."

Caden pointed the light through the entryway and revealed another hall that went on in darkness. "Seems safe enough." Cautious, she went forward, her handlight sweeping back and forth. A little further in, the path split off in three different directions. "Which way?"

Teddy knelt and studied the dust. "There are more than her footprints here," he said, waving his hand over the marks. "Either she's with someone, or someone's following her."

He pointed his light to the right. "This way."

Caden hurried forward. Someone was with her or following her. Either of those situations didn't sound good. With luck, whoever her sister traveled with had her best interests in mind. She didn't want to think about the alternative. Her hand clenched around her light. If they weren't lucky, someone else would not be either.

They came to a broad cement staircase with a metal bannister. She turned her light upward—nothing but steps.

"Onward and upward," Jolon complained with an enduring sigh.

Teddy went first, and Jolon after. Caden grasped the rail. She hated stairs. Most times straight walking didn't bother her though her muscles tired after a while and treated her to a dull ache. Steps, though—the bending of the knees—that hurt. With a slow inhale she thought of Deb and continued upward. The time to indulge in aching would have to come later.

The boys moved faster than her, but Jolon lagged. "How much farther?" he huffed as she came up beside him.

"Can't say," Teddy called down to them as he kept going.

Jolon puffed out his cheeks and whistled. "His legs keep growing longer, don't they? Pretty soon, he'll be nothing but legs and a blob of a head on the top. A couple of gangly arms sticking out the sides, but that's all."

She chuckled and smacked him on the back. "Come on, onward and upward."

"Onward and upward," he sighed but fell in step beside her.

"Come on you two," Teddy shouted, his voice reverberating down. "The air gets better up here."

Caden sped up, favouring her right leg as a pinching sharpness caught her in the knee. Better air, which was good. Two more levels and they caught up with Teddy as he stopped in front of an exit door.

"I tried a single finger push. Didn't move. We better put masks on."

She took a sniff. "But the air smells better, not so heavy."

"No sense taking a chance."

He sounded like Pa, which made her grin. She took her supplies off her back, rolling her shoulders to loosen tight neck muscles. After, she took out her respirator and slipped the mask on before turning the valve on the oxygen tank enough to let her breathe. The air hissed, and the metres fluctuated before holding steady.

The three of them nodded to each other. Teddy shoved on the silver bar that ran across the door, which creaked and opened a few inches. A stream of light spilled in, making them blink. Her brother put his shoulder to the door and pushed harder. It gave way, and he stumbled forward. A gush of chilly air rushed past them as the stairwell became bright. Caden caught his shirt and held on in case there wasn't anything beyond the door.

"It's okay, all is good," Teddy told her as he regained his feet. He checked his air quality gauge and removed his mask. "All good in all ways so far."

Caden slipped her mask, tank, and light back into her pack. Better safe than suffocating. She got that, but sometimes all the caution made their progress so slow.

They entered a wide hall containing little debris, but lots of dust. Two massive windows to their right revealed more fields of lumpy green dotted with broken buildings and rusting metal shells. After a quick glance outside, she examined the floor. Footsteps ran all over; some Deb sized, some larger.

"Where are we?" asked Jolon and Teddy shrugged.

"I should have brought the map."

"Let's go," she said, the pain in her leg getting worse.

"You okay?" asked Teddy when he noted her limp.

Annoyed with his concern, she mustered up a full fake smile. "Dandy. You?"

He gave a sharp exhale through pursed lips. "Right. We'll break later."

A loud bang surprised them.

"Where'd that come from?" Jolon asked under his breath.

"Come on," Caden ordered and hurried on.

Sounds of shuffling and excited voices got louder. Caden stumbled around a corner with the two boys behind her. "Deb! There you are!" she yelled as she caught sight of her sister.

The little girl squealed and danced about, a grin spread across her lips. She rushed toward them. "Hey, you found me!"

"Found you? You little...." Caden grabbed her and examined her everywhere. Dirt smudges covered her face, and a long tear cut her shirt, but otherwise she seemed fine. "What were you thinking?"

"She was thinking she was bored."

Caden glanced up sharply. "Cate."

Her old friend stepped out of the shadows of some pipes and boards. "Oh, yeah. You hit the target first try. Thought you were getting sloppy with all your..." she paused and rolled her one eye, "hominess."

"So, what? You thought it might be fun to take an eight-year-old kid into unexplored areas?" Teddy demanded as he put a hand on Deb's head.

Cate tossed back her hair and made her lips a thin line. "Yeah, that's me, exactly."

Caden stood. "Cate, no. You didn't." Deb tugged at her shirt, but she ignored her.

"Thanks, Cad, be on their side as usual."

Heat ran up Caden's neck. "What?"

"Cadie," Deb said, tugging harder.

"Let's go." Disapproval was clear on Teddy's face.

"No, Cad," her sister said louder, pulling on Caden's shirt.

"What?" she snapped.

Deb stared at her, wide-eyed before she stuck out her chin and put her hands on her hips, an almost perfect imitation of Teddy, who threw nasty eye-daggers at Cate.

"She found me."

Caden tilted her head. "What?"

Her little sister gestured toward Cate. "She found me. I didn't come here with her. I came here with me," she said with a defiant jab of her thumb toward her chest.

Disappointed, she crouched and held her sister's grey-eyed gaze. "Why? You know better. Deb, you understand it's not safe."

Her narrow shoulders shrugged. "I wanted an adventure. Teddy's always reading stories about adventures and I wanted one."

"See, hero, it's your fault," said Cate who stood with her arms crossed over her chest, but her hair covered much of her face—defense and offense, ready to take on the world or run in the other direction, whichever one came first.

"Sorry, Cate."

She dismissed her apology with a wave. "Like it matters."

As Caden got up, she nudged Teddy. Her brother scowled at her and rolled his eyes.

"Yeah, sorry."

"Oh, that was heartfelt," she laughed. "Try not to hurt yourself, hero."

"So what was the bang?"

Leave it to Jol to change the subject to get out of an awkward situation.

"We were playing tag, and the stuff fell over." Deb pointed toward a large sheet of broken wood. "You got food? I'm hungry."

He patted her on the head before dumping his stash on the floor and rummaging through the pockets. "Yep, somewhere in here."

Caden handed Deb her water bottle while Jolon gave her some potatocakes.

Teddy and Cate stared at each other, mirror images of stubbornness.

"Oh, they are the cutest couple," Jolon drawled, offering Caden a cake.

She took the food and sat down with him and Deb, spreading her legs out in front of her to ease her knees. "Oh, Jeeze," she spat and tugged on Teddy's pant leg. "Sit." She gestured to Cate. "You too. This doesn't need to be this awkward."

They both shuffled over like little children wary of each other. The scene was so ridiculous she almost laughed out loud. She handed them a potatocake each. Teddy snatched his, munching a portion as though eating was the most important thing to do.

Cate inspected her food as though she expected the mushed potato to bite back.

"So this alcove is where you've been hanging out these days?" she asked, trying to get her friend to relax.

"It works," Cate said and finally sampled her food.

"Anything interesting around here?" asked Teddy.

She snorted at him. "I tell you, and you tell everyone else, and those rag tags invade my space, and I'm out a home again."

"The other side has plenty of room..."

"Yeah, for them. Ample space for them." She thrust a hand toward the tower. "This place is mine. I found it. There's not much here for anyone, but this alcove is my home, got that?"

"This isn't my decision," he said, and Caden stared at him.

"No one needs to know, Teddy. She's right. We don't need the space yet and if this place has nothing anybody else wants, who cares?"

"Yeah, Ted. It's not like people need more stuff than what the mall provides," Jolon added.

"Not my decision," Teddy repeated with less conviction. He stood and dusted off his pants. "We should go."

"Teddy," Caden began, but Cate cut her off.

"You leave this alcove to me, and I'll take you somewhere special."

They all turned toward her. She shuffled her feet but clenched her jaw. "I found a place, a good place here. Not much use to me, but you'll love it. You leave this area alone, and I'll give you that place."

"What kind of place?" Caden asked.

"We can't bargain for areas. We're not Upperlords staking out territory." Despite Teddy's insistence, he shifted from foot to foot, twitching with curiosity.

Cate thrust her hands against her waist and faced Teddy. "I won't tell you, any of you if you won't vow to give this space to me."

"What's so enticing about this?" Teddy waved a hand about. "This is a cement alcove in a defective building. There are lots of areas like this."

"So what does it matter if I make this mine?" she demanded back, meeting him inch for inch.

They glared at each other, neither wanting to back down.

"I vow." Deb got to her feet and stood beside Cate. "I won't tell no one." With her little face stern, she turned to Teddy. "An he won't neither."

"Eh, me too," Jolon grunted as he got up. "Don't see much reason not to."

Teddy turned from one to the other, his face flushed. "Fine," he said, throwing his hands up. "But they'll find out at some point."

"Not if we fix it so they can't." Caden grinned at her brother. "Come on, Teddy. Don't pretend we haven't done something like this before. The warehouse hid tunnels for years. No one will care about a small area like this."

With a stubborn thrust of his chin, he crossed his arms over his chest. "I said fine."

Deb made a Ma-like gesture. "Yeah, but you didn't vow."

They all laughed, and he gave in. "Fine, I vow to tell no one of Cate's area. Does that satisfy, little Ma?" he said, ruffling her hair.

"All good," she declared and grabbed Teddy and Cate's hands and stuck them together. "Now shake."

The two of them stood still as though electrified before stepping away from each other. Caden smiled to herself and glanced over at Jolon who turned his eyes upward but smirked at her as though it was sickening but inevitable.

After sitting for so long on the floor, her joints stiffened up and protested when she went to stand. The others were kind enough not to say anything, but she sensed their concern and sighed, tired of such loving pity.

The bookstore was an extensive building, which echoed emptiness with such volume, the silence made Caden's ears ache. She always found empty places sad as they perched on the narrow edge of existing—neglected and lacking interaction—covered in dust, which got into spaces left too long, as though time took their energy. Streams of light came down from a few windows high on the walls. Other lower windows lined one wall, but were black with dirt and debris—probably buried deep underground during the initial environmental upheaval—a few of them cracked, and some shattered, letting piles of earth in. Otherwise, the place wasn't in too bad.

Excitement raced through Teddy like electricity, his eyes open so wide they almost took up his whole face. He jogged through row after row, his handlight flitting about, helping him explore his new treasures. Every page he touched seemed to vibrate in his hands as though waiting for him.

"Doesn't take much to make him happy." Cate leaned against the side of a shelf and ran a finger over the line of books.

Her expression was one of envy. Why would she envy Teddy? His home, his health? No, she never seemed to care about those things, and she was healthier than most people, except for her missing eye. Yes, she was plain, solid and strong, but also feminine like one of the stone statues in the sunroom.

"Yeah, he's always been an optimistic bugger," Caden searched for a stool.

"Leg bugging ya?"

She grunted and settled herself on the steps that led down to a colourful area of stuffed animals and colourful books. "Careful, Deb," she called as her little sister plunged into a mound of fluffy creatures. "You don't know what might live in there."

"Don't think much ever lived in here." Cate sat beside her. "The place was pretty well sealed, and there's not much to attract anything except paper."

"I found cookies," said Jolon, who had wandered off to a section of pots, vases, and other household items behind them. "And chocolate in tins. Some teas too."

"Perfect, now all we need is water and a stove," Cate said with her usual touch of sarcasm.

Caden hid a slight grin. "You, though, you are the exact opposite to Teddy."

The other girl nudged her in the ribs. "And you're wishy inside now. You would have had the perfect quip to cut him to pieces in the past. Now, well..."

"Well, what?"

"You're all quiet and unaffected." Her mouth turned down, and her eyes tightened as though she felt abandoned.

"I guess." Caden studied her hands. They pulsed with a dull ache at the joints. Being on guard, expecting hurt, and bracing herself for every eventuality exhausted her. Her body contained enough pain; she was finished with making more. "Never helped me much to be cynical, I guess. Things don't seem to be that important anymore."

"That sounds depressing. You all right?"

"Am I all right as in 'cutting the life-string? Yes," she said with a droll sigh. "Nor am I contemplating taking the long fall into a pit or snagging a mean necklace. Don't throw Undercity suicide phrases at me."

Her friend's lips twisted into a wry grimace. "I'm not. Hate those sayings. Always found them curious as a kid, but that's before I realized what they meant. So, how are you in a 'I plan to live forever' way?'"

"I'm good," she said with a small smile. "Actually, I'm terrific. I guess I got a sampling of peace and found the flavour yummy."

Cate blew a sharp gust of air through her lips. "Sounds dull—for me, at least. It's good for you. You're kind of a..." she paused, her eye twinkling.

"A what?"

"A mush under all that tough," she said with a snicker.

"Yeah? Give me a moment and I'll show you who's a mush," Caden retorted with a grin and pinch to her arm.

"Oww," Cate yelped and rubbed her arm, exaggerating the pain for effect.

Teddy wandered by, his arms full of books.

"We'll never get him out of here now."

Cate laughed. "He is a brain boy, isn't he?"

"Always with his head in the books. I think knowledge makes him feel safe, gives him boundaries. We all build our own walls."

"Bet the girls think he's the catch," she said, making a face.

"Some of the boys too," Caden said with a nod.

"Not you, though."

Caden turned toward her friend, the glint in her eye hinted at hopeful. "Yeah, no. You'll get no competition from me. He'll only ever be my brother. Can't think of him any other way. Don't think he could think of me in any other way either. We're too brother and sistery."

Cate gaped at her. "Competition? I've no interest in him!" she insisted, jabbing a digit in Teddy's direction.

"Ah, huh. I believe you, no, I do," Caden laughed.

Her friend made a face and smacked her arm. "Stop."

"Hey, mean," she said, rubbing her arm.

"Sorry." Cate clasped her hands in her lap. "Didn't think I hit that hard."

Caden got up, stretching with care. "Yeah, well, I'm made of paper, remember? One touch and I crumple. Let's get some of that food before Jolon eats his way through everything."

They wound through the tables stacked with nick-knacks and shelves filled with books. There seemed to be texts on everything, at least, the covers had pictures of almost everything. She paused and picked up a picture of a woman holding a flower in her hand. Caden flipped through the pages, but the words twisted around in a blur of black wiggles.

"Hey, you want me to read that one to you?"

She turned and grinned at Teddy. "Some day," she said, putting the novel back and nodding toward the stack in his arms. "I would say you have enough to keep you busy here for a while."

"Ah, yeah," he said with a happy, but shy grin. "So much is here; it's exciting. This room holds a world of information, literally."

"You are so weird." Cate hooked her hands on her pockets as she took a casual stance against a bookshelf.

He glanced at her and shook his head, his eyes tightening. "You might think that, but I don't. We have a whole village of people who need this knowledge. We have books on building stuff, survival, medicine, everything. This could save us."

"Right, we could use them for fuel when the electrical stuff runs out," Cate retorted and turned away.

"Your friend is..."

"Stupid. Don't say it. She isn't," Caden interrupted, angry at his judgement of Cate. "You don't know her. She's scared that's all."

"I was going to say stubborn," Teddy continued. "I can tell she's far from stupid." He turned and left in a snit.

Caden buried an aggravated howl and caught up with Cate. "He just wants to..."

"Save everybody. He's got that whole responsibility thing on him like a coat." Cate stopped and took a mug with a kitten sprawled across the surface off of one display.

"Yeah, that about sums him up."

"And he's right," she went on under her breath. She placed the cup back down and tossed her hair back, exposing her closed eye socket. The dark lid sunk down. "I can't read much, but I know enough stories to know the heroes don't go for the girl without two sparkling sweet eyes that glow in the moonlight so, no. I'm not interested in him either."

"Perfect, we're a pair, you and me, and...." she gave the mug back to Cate, "a cat or ten." Caden laughed and took her friend's arm. She didn't believe her, though. Teddy wasn't that shallow and too many sparks flew between them to be indifference—perhaps enemies, but not indifferent.

They found Jolon at a corner table, his feet propped up and an array of goodies before him. He had his elbow propped against the table as he put a cookie in his mouth. His other hand held a colourful book he read by the light of several candles he collected on his table.

"Give over." Cate pulled the chair out from Jolon's feet, passed the wooden seat over to Caden, and took another one for herself.

"Rude, that's what you are," Jolon muttered and offered Caden a biscuit. "They're pretty good."

"Thanks." Caden fished her bottle of water out of her pack. She poured some into Cate's mug and took some for herself. "Where's Deb?"

The others shrugged.

"Probably still lost in all those toys," Cate said, tearing open a wrapper.

"I'll get her," Jolon sighed as though he was old and weary. He dropped his book and wandered away.

"Why that alcove?" Caden asked now that they were alone.

"Eh, doesn't have to be," Cate admitted between bites. "I just... he annoyed me, I guess. He stood in my find and claimed everything for his own as though he had the right. It pissed me off." She laughed at her confession, blushing. "I do want my own place, though. Some area that I can protect as my own."

"You could find that in the tower."

"Yeah, if I want to tow along with everyone else."

"What's wrong with that? Alone isn't so wonderful either."

Cate took a swallow of her water and tucked her hair back behind her ear. "It's easier," she admitted in a quiet voice.

Caden nodded. Yes, alone was easier than forgiving, forgetting, caring, and sharing. She shuttered. "Yeah, but it's alone."

Her friend kept her attention elsewhere. She understood. The tunnel rats and creepers were never easy to avoid in Undercity.

"Guess what I found," shouted a delighted Deb as she and Jolon came up.

She turned in her chair. Her little sister had a ball of grey fur in her arms. At first, she thought the creature was a stuffed kitten, but the grey ball moved and meowed, wrapping fuzzy paws around Deb's fingers.

"A bunch of them roam the place, plus one snarling, nasty mamma who I think, owns this place. Now I get why this place has no mice. The storage room in the back is kitty heaven, years' worth. I figure they prowl through the ventilation system too. They are probably spread out all over this area," Jolon told them. "She cornered this one in a cupboard. I don't think she means to let the poor animal go."

"Ma won't let you keep it," Teddy said, joining them. He had a book tucked under one arm and petted the kitten with his other hand.

"Yes she will, she's always said a cat would be useful," Deb told him, hugging her kitty.

Yes, for food, Caden mused, but she didn't mention that to her sister.

"Don't worry, kid. If your ma doesn't let you keep kitty, you can leave her with me and come visit," Cate said, sticking her tongue out at Teddy.

He frowned and took a seat on the other side of the table, helping himself to the food.

Caden held out her hands. "Give the kitty to me. You come eat and drink some water."

Deb gave over her pet with reluctance. The little thing mewed and complained before settling down as Caden stroked the animal into submission. The creature's purr was rough, as though its engine could not quite get going. "What you going to call it?"

"Mr. Poufy," Deb said with a chocolate cookie grin.

Silence took over the library when everyone left, so Cate wandered back to her alcove. Deb took the kitty, hoping her mother would let her keep Mr. Poufy, and Caden said she planned to come back and visit tomorrow. That probably meant her brothers too, and that made Cate itchy like she had an allergy rash.

As she leaned against the window and stared out at the world beyond, placed her fingers on the glass. Grassy mounds of earth reached up to the sill, leaving the view clear. The sun sat low on the horizon, turning everything a dusty purple. She liked sunsets; that was one of the few things she appreciated about leaving Undercity.

Life improved for most people, well, for everyone, but also brought new dangers. People no longer focused on survival day in and out. Now they had time to be more carnal, and she had no interest in anything like that. It didn't matter. She had her own protected little area.

As she turned away from the window, she crossed her arms and surveyed her new rooms. The place seemed bare but had only two doors, one leading to the towers and the other to the library. She could secure the one and use the other for an escape if the first failed.

Darkness painted gloomy shadows everywhere. She flicked on the handlight Caden left her. If she brought some stuff up, she could curtain off a part for a sleeping area and throw cushions in a corner for a comfy space. With any luck, she could convince a cat or two to keep her company and get rid of any rats or mice.

She shuddered. Even though she grew up in the tomb of Undercity where some people ate rats as a regular meal, she hated the things. To her, the disgusting, gross creatures only made people sick and ruined stuff.

As she hummed an abstract tune to herself, she sauntered to the bookstore. The place was silent except for the rustling of cats. She never saw them before, but she didn't stay in the building long. The rows of books disturbed her. They were a massive unknown she didn't know how to bridge. Teddy read. That annoyed her. He had something she didn't. He would teach her if she asked, but that was the problem. She would have to ask, and he was so arrogant, so sure of himself.

Yes, he and his family found their new home. Yes, they saved everyone, well, most everyone from the Upperlords, but still. He wasn't perfect. His hair was more messy brown than straight black though he had pleasant eyes. He was tall enough but too boney.

She blew her bangs out of her vision and went back to the decorative side of the shop. Some fuzzy and kitten-soft cushions and blankets lay stacked up on a display. She spread a blanket out, piled a bunch of pillows on top, and tied everything into a bundle.

Next, she gathered up cups and dishes, which would be good if she found water, although she could get some from the tower. It irked her to still rely on them, but at the moment, she had little choice. As she searched around, she caught movement out of the corner of her eye. She froze and listened, but the place was quiet, even the cats didn't seem to be around. Carefully, she turned and faced her image locked in a mirror framed in decorated metal.

She bent closer, the darkness subduing her image. Was she pretty? She heard people say she had a certain amount of appeal. Her complexion was a soft gold, not pale like Deb or deep brown like Caden, but somewhere in between, and her hair waved out in a pile of orange-red. She preferred it that way; it covered her face.

Leaning closer, she stared deep into her green eye all flecked with bits of gold and surrounded by long, straight lashes—did she resemble her Pa or Ma? Like most of those down in the pits, her lineage was a vague concept. Mrs. Fish suggested her father was an Upperlord, but she doubted the accuracy of the claim. Her Ma died of food poisoning after she ate a half-cooked rat. Cate didn't remember her too much. After, she bunked with Caden, who stayed with her aunt until she died of fever. Everyone always died of some dreadful fever or worse in the stinking, rotting pits. Forty was old in Undercity.

She dug in her pocket and pulled out the blue marble she found in the fountain. The glass orb seemed big enough and had a deep, sparkling quality. She stared at herself in the mirror, pulling back her hair from her empty eye socket. It took effort, but she got the lid to move. Tentatively, she pulled the lid up, revealing the hollow space below. Skin grew over the back, smooth and thick. She took a deep breath and held the marble up to her face.

Would it hurt?

She swallowed hard and pushed. The blue stone fell into the cavity, and she let the lid go down. Her tear ducts watering. She hated that crying came easy even though she had no eye. As she puffed out a laboured breath, she peered closer at her reflection. Either the mirror had evil warping powers, or she looked ridiculous. The lid wouldn't sit right, and the marble was too small. She popped it out and chucked the orb aside, wiping her tears with her sleeve. She let her hair fall back over her face. What a pathetic, useless idea.

Dejected, she tossed the mirror aside. After selecting a few more things, a vase for water and a box for her more precious items, she hunted for some cloth suitable for her monthly. The whole process was a tedious chore to clean up after but didn't happen often. For some, monthlies never came at all. She wasn't certain if that was a blessing or a curse. At least, if anyone cornered them, they never worried about ending up pregnant.

She pondered her pile when she finished and realized she would need to make several trips unless she found a cart. She gazed about with her handlight before her. Perhaps something hid in the storage room. Leaving her stuff behind, she went into the back where a horrible stench assaulted her nose. She found stacks of stuff everywhere; mostly books, boxes, and such. Some of the shelves fell over limiting moving space and cats crawled everywhere. It was amazing they hadn't spread out into the rest of the building. An echoing bang made her swirl around, her light swinging with her. A mangy black tabby jumped from out of the tin air vent and wandered off into another lower down.

With a heavy exhale she relaxed her shoulders—annoying animals. She climbed over some books and moved aside a desk, resuming her search for a cart. As she moved around a shelving unit piled high with bags and boxes, she found a solid door of grey metal with a bar across the middle. She stared, wondering where it led. Nowhere? Outside? It might be stuck or buried like most of the other exits on this level. Her fingers and her curiosity twitched.

The door was the type with a quick closure, limiting her exposure to anything dangerous. She crept up to the opening and put her ear to the cool surface, listening. The sound of her beating heart thudded against the metal. With a lick to her lips, she put her hand to the bar and controlled her breathing. That's how she found the alcove and the bookstore. This was the same.

She took a deep breath and pushed. A light gust of air caressed her as the door opened. The breeze blew strands of her hair back and made her close her eye for a moment. Hesitant, she opened her eye again and pointed her light through. She didn't see much. Unable to resist anymore, she gasped and tried to ease into breathing. The air stung with staleness, but seemed okay. A cat ran across her feet, and she yelped, dropping her light.

"Mean thing," she muttered and scrambled for the handlight. A few more cats ran back and forth. If the area was safe for them, it might be okay for her. She stepped through the door and pivoted her light about.

The spot seemed unremarkable, dirty and wide. Rats scurried everywhere. A rush of assorted cats went after them, yowling in their hunt. The ground was grey cement with greasy, oily stains covering everywhere. The wall in front of her was brick and the two to the left and the right were rubble. She shined her light toward the roof, which was several floors up. Beams and rubble made up the ceiling, caved in walls that should have fallen all the way down, but somehow got stuck and buried.

A metal object stood a few feet from her and reflected her light. Curious, she went over, watching for rats. It was orange under all the dirt, with windows and rubber wheels. What its purpose was, she couldn't say, but she figured Teddy would tell her. The idea sat ill in her stomach. If she asked, he'd explain whatever she wanted to understand. He taught Deb. The kid might help her in secret and one day she might surprise him. "Oh, that book? Read it. Sorry, Teddy, a little boring. I prefer this one instead."

The image made her chuckle. She explored the location more, avoiding the rubble walls in case something gave way. Another door across the way stood open with a skeleton in ragged clothes in the way. Grimacing, she stepped over it and into a stairwell. She swung her light around. Up or down? Down appeared grim and unsettling—she was tired of down. Up ended in a busted landing. The door across from her presented the easier option.

Her eye stung, and she pressed her palm against the lid. The day had to be late, and fatigue pulled at her. A cat meowed at her feet and rubbed against her leg.

"Well, Kitty, what do you think? Should we try one more?"

The animal wound around her leg and flicked her tail. She took another breath and shoved at the door. It swung open into a hall with the usual swoosh of air. The fearless creature trotted in as though it was home. If it could breathe, she could breathe, and she exhaled.

Doors lined both sides of the hallway similar to the ones in Caden's home. She checked each one as she walked. Locked. The kitty ran ahead of her, disappearing through an open door.

"Where you going, kitty? You don't know what's in there," she said, her voice muted in the chilly air. A swirl of wind brushed over her. She blinked rapidly. The air held a fresh scent with a hint of perfume like the bottled stuff from one of the store stalls, but nicer. Curious, she followed. Her heart skipped a beat as she stared at the room before her. It had a kitchen off to her left with a stove and everything, and an open room in front set out with comfortable furniture.

Her breath escaped her, and she gaped at an open glass door, exposing her to the elements. Stunned, she stepped forward, her hand extended and trembling.

The cat meowed again and went outside. Outside, she went numb. Outside—half of her expected to expire in seconds. The other half of her wanted to run and close the door, never to open it again. All of her kept going forward until she stood one step away from leaving the building.

Darkness hung out there like a shroud. She couldn't see much even with her handlight. As far as she could tell, a patch of grass covered mossy cement blocks and leaves covered the walls. The fuzzy feline called to her, but she moved away. This was more than she could take all in one night.

"Come on, kitty, come back," she called, her nerve giving out. "I'm shutting the door, fluff ball. Move or suffer." The stubborn animal just stared at her then rolled in the grass. Cate shoved the door shut and collapsed against the glass, panting. A tear wet her cheek, and a trembling ache rushed through her muscles, she backed away and stumbled against the couch, falling onto the soft cushions. She pulled the blanket strewn across the back over her body and curled up, shivering. Confused, she stared at the glass door until her eye closed. Numb, she fell into a troubled sleep filled with dangerous dreams.

Light shone on her face in the morning, waking her. Warm and comfortable, she stretched and fell off her bed as she remembered where she was. She lay on the tan carpet and stared at the door. The cat stood on the other side of the glass, meowing to get in.

She got up and went to the glass awed by the view. The courtyard reached about twenty feet across and thirty feet deep with high walls covered in draping vines. As the sunlight crept in, the blossoms twisted with life. Huge flowers of blue, purple, and red unfolded, turning their faces toward the light. Cate stared, glued to the magic occurring right before her. Enthralled, she drew the door open, barely aware of the kitty pawing at her ankle. She stepped out. Some time in the night she had kicked off her shoes, and now her bare feet sank into the turf. It was chilly and wet, sending shivers up her spine. The scent of the vegetation filled the surrounding air.

Her heart quickened. She was outside and breathing. She stood outside with the sun touching her skin.

"Ahhhhh." Panicked, she ran back into the apartment. She jumped up and down, laughing and shaking. Panting, she stopped and stared at the flowers again, pushing her hair out of her view.

"Oh, oh, oh," she exclaimed, waving her hands as she paced. The cat came back in and wove around her ankles. "I gotta tell someone. No. I can't tell anyone. Why? Why not? Ahhh!"

She scooped up the kitty. This was hers, her magic spot. "I'll tell them, I will. Not yet, though. Don't know if it's safe. They're okay. They like their tower."

"Ow," she yelped as the kitty nibbled her finger. "Okay, yes. They might help me figure that out, but they might take it away from me too, and you wouldn't want that would you?" she said as she rubbed under the animal's chin. "No, they can be daring and walk out a door or open a window. This is mine, ours, for the moment."

Her pet leapt out of her arms and ran out into the open. With her hands extended in front of her, she went out again and stood in amid the beauty of nature. She raised her face to the sky and let the light touch her. Her eye closed, and she swayed with the wind, feeling fully alive for the first time.

Chapter 3

Once the chores for the day were done, the three of them slipped away back to the bookshop. They packed up food and water, enough for a long day, and Caden made certain to bring enough for Cate too.

"I believe he was hoping you would spend the day with him," Teddy told her while they wrapped up some potatocakes.

Confused, Caden turned in the direction he gestured. Henri stood in the doorway to the kitchen, shifting and twitching. His face lit up as he saw her turn his way. She dropped her gaze and kept on packing.

"Come on, you can't blame him for liking you. At least, talk to him."

Grunting, she nodded and pushed her stash toward him. "Fine, you can carry this too," she said and went toward Henri, who got more fidgety as she got closer. "Hi," she said, trying to keep an arm's length between them.

"Hi." He played with a navy hat with white pin striping and a narrow brim in his hand. As clever as the item was, she hoped it wasn't another present. "Found this. What you think?" he asked as he plopped it on his head. His grin was so silly she couldn't help smiling.

"Looks good."

"Yeah?"

"Yeah." She nibbled on her lower lip, trying to make up an excuse to deter him from spending the day with her. "So, I got..."

"I wanted do something special today, but can't," he interrupted all in a rush. He gestured toward the tunnel entrance and hit his hand against the doorframe in the process. "Some kind noise on other side and I gotta check things out with your Pa and others."

"What kind of noise?" Teddy asked.

The brute shrugged. "Might be shifting, might be digging."

Teddy twitched. The wheels turned in his brain with the internal fight between his curiosity and his thirst for books. "It's probably nothing."

"Yeah," he said, but he didn't sound convinced.

"Hey, it's not like they would burst through like rats from a rotten cardboard box. Let's go explore and find out what Pa says tonight," she suggested, not wanting to spend her day waiting around to see if a wall was going to fall down.

"What's up?" Jolon asked as he joined them.

"Some action at the old entrance has Henri on duty," Teddy said, still shifting uneasily.

Jolon made a face. "What kind of action? 'The world is shifting, as usual, action' or 'bloody hell; they're coming to get us' action?"

"Good question," Caden replied. "They're not sure." She waved a hand toward Teddy. "He's fluctuating between worlds now. Books or tunnels, which will win out?"

Teddy leaned from one foot to another and ran a hand through his hair. "Okay, we'll keep to our original plan, but, Henri, we'll meet you tonight, okay? You're my eyes and ears in this."

The brute nodded, and his forest green eyes shifted to Caden. She managed what she hoped was a friendly, but not encouraging, grin. He appeared confused, but nodded and left.

"Gah, what happened to our happy group?" Jolon said as they went back to their packs.

"What are you babbling about?" Caden asked, slinging her pack on.

"All this romance and dopy eyes. Two seconds and you guys are in mushland. It's kinda revolting," he told her, scrunching his face in disgust.

Both she and Teddy protested.

"I'm not getting mushy," Caden insisted, waving a hand toward where Henri had been. "He's the one mushing."

"I'm ignoring you," Teddy said and walked off.

"Sure, run away." Jolon laughed and followed. "Mushy, mushy, mushy," he said, ending in kissing sounds.

Caden moved in behind him and thwacked him on the back of the head. "Grow up."

"Oww, hey," Jolon growled, rubbing his head. "I've got no hair to soften your affectionate aggression."

When they got the alcove, they found, to their surprise, the door blocked. Teddy hammered with a closed fist. "Hey, Cate, open up."

"Cate, you home?" Caden hollered.

A shuffling and a bang occurred before the door opened. Cate met them with a disapproving scowl but stepped aside to let them in. The place was different. Blankets hung across one corner, and several pillows gathered in another. With the sun filtering in, the area was cozy.

"Hey," Caden greeted with an amicable grin.

Cate said hey back, but avoided eye contact. Something was up. She was more nervous than usual, as though something had happened, which changed her life.

"You guys took your time getting here," she said as she backed away from them.

"Didn't know you expected us at a specific time," Teddy said, his posture defensive.

"Ooh, sunshine and roses, life with you guys is a bundle of crumbled cookies," Jolon mocked. "Let's go. I need to find something more interesting to do than witness you two flirting."

"Shut up, Jol," Teddy retorted and stomped off toward the bookstore.

Cate gave them both dirty glares and fell in with Caden. They walked on for quite a while, and the boys got a fair way ahead of them.

"So, what's up?" asked Caden, and Cate glanced toward her.

"What?"

"Hey, I know you. Something's shifted. Give. Is it Teddy?"

"Gahh, would you all drop the Teddy thing? Life is more than a cute guy with a swelled head," she replied with a roll of her eye.

"Okay, so what is up?" Caden pushed.

Cate fidgeted and twisted a strand of her hair. "Nothing. At least, nothing yet. I'll tell you if anything changes." She stopped at the entrance to the store and turned toward Caden. "Do I seem different?"

"Yeah, you look like you are hiding a secret," Caden said, stopping with her.

"Aside from that," she said with an irritated wave of her hand.

Caden examined her up and down. "No, you seem the same as yesterday, why?"

Cate let out a long exhale. "It's nothing. I just...I can't say. I'll explain when I know, okay?"

"Guess so." Caden moved around her and into the building. "Makes me curious, but I can wait. Just tell me if it's anything serious like you're dying or something."

"Yeah, sure," she answered with a small smile as she relaxed in her posture. "Hey, where's the kid?"

"Deb? Ma wanted her home today. She's supposed to play with a few kids her age for once."

They stopped at a pair of comfy looking chairs and sprawled out in them.

"Are there many?" Cate asked, snuggling into an overstuffed corner of her seat. "Kids her age, that is."

Caden put her feet up and relaxed. "Probably about a dozen or so. Teddy has a better record of them. He's trying to start a school, but it's a slow go."

"Why?"

She shrugged. "Some of the parents don't see a point. Some of the kids don't either. The older ones would rather scrounge for stuff or goof off with each other. Resources are few too." She gazed around at the abundance of books. "He has all this now, so it might get better."

"The numbers are dwindling, aren't they?" Cate asked after a moment.

"What numbers?"

"The numbers of people."

Caden nodded. "Yeah. I think there is a handful of kids younger than Deb, and I've heard of two pregnancies from Ma. The hope is things will improve now."

"Do you want kids?"

She glared at her friend. "Don't you start."

"Start what?" Cate asked, innocently putting her hands in front of her.

"Start going on about me and...." she shut her mouth, wishing to avoid the topic of Henri.

Cate sat up and leaned in close, a sly grin on her face. "And who."

"Nobody."

"I wasn't asking if you had a boyfriend. I wanted to know if you wanted to have kids," Cate told her as she sat back again.

"Guess so, sort of," Caden admitted with a small shrug. "It's so hard to think about stuff so huge in this life. It's like wishing for miracles. I'm glad when I wake up with another day to get through." Cate curled up, hugging her knees with a thoughtful glance to her. "What about you? Do you want kids?"

She shrugged a shoulder. "Perhaps. I suppose children would be kinda cool, but I'm not sure I'm the mothery type. I like being on my own too much. Maybe later, if life gives us a later."

"Some of the elders are saying everyone needs to have more babies for the survival of our people," Caden said, grimacing. "I understand, but it seems the majority of the risk and burden falls on the women."

"Yeah, it's a fine line. They can't force women to get pregnant, though." She scowled. "Well, in a way they can."

"I can't see things ever getting so ugly. There are too many good people like Pa and Ma around to let things get so bad. Besides, I don't think people aren't trying; I think people can't."

Cate clapped her hands against her legs and sat up. "Well, this is getting depressing. We should do something more productive."

"I liked what you were doing with the alcove. This will be a comfortable home when you get the space all together."

Her friend shifted, so her hair fell in front of her eye. "It will do for now. Let's find your brainy brother. He's been quiet, so he's either been eaten by books or fell asleep."

They found Teddy at a long table surrounded by piles of books. Caden shifted some to the side and found a seat.

"Hey, don't touch those," Teddy exclaimed, looking up for a rather large journal. "I stacked them in order."

"Oh, I moved them an inch. Don't fall apart. Your order is still intact. Though what that order is, is beyond me." She perused a thin book with a cartoon of a bear on the cover, flipping through the pages. The words meant little, so she ignored them, enjoying the pictures instead.

"What are these?" Cate asked, holding up a strange looking book. "This has nothing inside, but this disk thing. How do you read that?"

"It's called an audio book," Teddy replied, sitting back in his chair. "They recorded people reading a book. It plays on some machine, and you can listen to the book."

Caden put her picture book aside and grabbed one of the audio books, turning it over in her hands. "That would be fun. I like listening to stories."

"Yeah, but I haven't been able to find one of the players. One of the stores had a bunch of similar disks, which are supposed to contain music, but I can't find anything to make them work either."

"If you found something, how would you power it," Cate asked, placing her audio book back.

He smiled at her. "Exactly. Some of the power stuff, like lights, we've figured out, but there's still so much we don't understand. The kitchen has machines Ma and the others would love to use, but there are gaps in our knowledge." He gestured at all the books. "That's what I'm hoping to do here, fill those gaps."

"How do you do that? Fill the gaps," she asked.

"How can we help?" Caden added, with a nod to Cate, who gave her an outraged glare.

Teddy got up from his chair. "Come with me," he said and strode off toward Deb's favourite area.

"Hate him or love him, I don't care," she whispered as they trailed after him. "You're involved. If helping him keeps you from being alone, I'm in."

"Why is it so important to you?"

"Shhh," she said as her brother stopped.

"This is the kids' area," he said, turning in a circle and gesturing to the racks. Each shelf was colourful, stuffed with bright characters, animals, and toys. "The books here start at the basics. We can use these to teach people." His eyes shone as he spoke, his cheeks flushing with excitement. "I didn't know where to start. When I went to school, we had few resources, so my teacher went with what we had. That's what made things so challenging for people; learning wasn't gradual. These books go in a sensible order and fill in the missing spaces." He rushed over to a shelf and pulled out a book, flipping the pages at them. "These show you how to read and write." He grabbed another one. "These show you numbers, and these," he snatched up yet another, "are all about how things work. We can start at the beginning and re-create our world. We might even find a way to live outside, away from these walls."

Silence fell on the bookstore. Outside—a tempting, scary, and desperately terrifying idea. Caden wanted to both run away and celebrate.

"So, what do we do?" she asked, glancing toward Cate, who seemed quiet and unsettled. Caden figured she must be as fearful of the aspect of stepping outdoors as herself. It made sense. They had grown up in the worst of the worst, and it was all they knew.

"Well, at first, I thought we could make the school in the sunshine room where everything is bright and all. But the space is best for growing what food we can, so I guess that won't work. The tower has several rooms big enough with tables and chairs for everyone, but the resources are here." He shifted a quick glance at Cate as though preparing for war. "So I thought it would be best to set up the school here."

"What?" Cate demanded as though his words interrupted her thoughts and sunk in.

"The school? We could set it up here."

"Here. Perfect, except for the fact they need to go through my home to get here." Aggravated, she slapped her hand against her thigh.

He shifted on his feet. "Yes, I realize that."

"And you think that's fine, hey?"

"No," he began, pushing his hand through his hair. "I mean..."

"You mean? What do you mean? You mean it's okay for people traipsing through my life, invading my privacy for your precious school. Just so you can be in charge of something."

That did it. He puffed up, all red and indignant. "Just so...just so..." he sputtered and slammed his book down. "This isn't about me. This is about everyone. You're the one who is self-focused. How dare we invade your space to make everyone else's lives a little better."

"Whoa, people, calm down." Caden put her hands up between them. "This doesn't need to go this way."

"She's impossible," Teddy snapped, and crossed his arms in front of his chest.

"Me?" she barked, jabbing her thumb against her chest. "You're the one who can't even say 'please.' You think you're so amazing. That you found this wonderful life for everyone, but you don't consider how hard it might be to be ripped out of everything familiar and end up, end up..." She turned away.

Annoyed, Caden scowled at Teddy and shoed him away. He threw his hands up, his expression confused and sorry, before he stomped away. She turned back to her friend and stood close, knowing better than to make physical contact.

"Hey, I don't remember much about the day we all moved. I know I wasn't feeling too well, bit of a fever. It was all rush and blur."

Cate shuddered. "I remember everyone pushing about, crowding into the tunnels like rats running away from a flood. I left everything behind. Everything I claimed as me and mine is all back in the little space I made mine rotting away. Someone else has probably taken it over by now."

"Yeah, but things are better here. You must see that."

Her friend nodded and took a deep inhale. "Yeah, I do. For most people." A tight grimace spread on her lips as she shook her head. "For me too, I know. And you. You look better than you have in a long time, and that's worth a lot."

They shared a chuckle and Caden nudged her friend. "Yeah, well Teddy isn't so bad; his school thing is a good idea."

"Don't push," Cate said, rolling her eye. "But, yes, as annoying as it might be to admit, it's a good idea. Just don't tell him I said so."

"I won't, promise," Caden agreed with a grin.

For the next couple of hours, Teddy set them to finding and piling together all the supplies needed to put a school together. He and Cate called an unspoken truce even managed a level of politeness to each other.

All afternoon, they worked at a steady pace and Cate was getting sleepy. After a while, they sat at a table and spread out some food. The room was so hot and stuffy now, with little airflow. She pressed her hands against her face, her one eye burning. The urge to share her experience outside—how fresh and good the air was—squirmed in her. It couldn't be bad. She felt fine. Caden said she looked fine, so it had to be safe. She should tell them, would tell them. Placing her arms on the cluttered table, she opened her mouth, but the words got stuck in her throat. Instead, she pretended to yawn. It was hers for a little while longer; she needed it to be hers.

"We should check if we can connect the ventilation system in the tower to this building," Teddy decided, yawning too. "The air is stale. We'll also need power and lights. Water too, if possible."

"Seems this is more work than moving the supplies." Caden munched on a cracker and stuck her legs on another chair.

Cate gave an inward sigh of relief, figuring if she had said that, Teddy would have dismissed the idea as her being selfish. She picked at a potatocake and kept herself out of the conversation.

"True," Teddy admitted with a grimace. "Either way, this will be work. I guess we could search around the hotel and see if there is any place suitable to make a permanent space."

Caden and Cate shared hopeful smile.

"I'm sure there must be," Caden continued. "Then we could use this place as a new trip or adventure to get kids excited."

"Hey, yeah," Cate said, forgetting to keep herself neutral. "They could come here on their first day of classes and pick out their books and supplies. The little kids would love it."

"And you could help," Teddy slipped in and took a sip of water.

She tightened her gaze. "Ah, ha. Good try."

He shrugged. "Hey, I'll take any help I can get."

"Yeah, well, appreciate what you're getting now and leave signing me up for anything else till later."

"I'll take that as a maybe," he replied with a light snicker and a nod. "Which is better than a no."

She shook her head at him. "How can that be better than a no? We don't get along. To you, I'm selfish and insensitive and to me, you're arrogant and egotistical. Why do you even want to work with me?"

He grinned and linked his hands behind his head. "Because you use words like arrogant and egotistical. In other words, you are smart. You pick things up and interpret them into your life."

"I don't read," she said, putting his compliments aside.

"You could," he said with a tilt of his head. "I don't think it would take you much."

She jerked her thumb at him and said to Caden, "He's got a one-track mind, doesn't he? Read, read, read, everyone must read."

Her friend gave her a small smile, her gaze dropping to the table. "Yeah."

In a moment, Cate understood reading was a skill Caden always saw as beyond her. She grimaced, realizing she stepped into a mess.

"Okay, fine. You teach me to read, and I'll practice reading to Cad. How's that?" she offered without thinking about what she suggested.

"Deal," Teddy declared, putting out a hand.

Cate raised a sceptical eyebrow, but Caden grinned. "Fine," she said and shook his hand.

"Perfect, I'll get a workbook. We can start right away," Teddy said before rushing off.

She flicked a finger toward her friend. "The things I go through for you."

Caden laughed. "Right, use me as an excuse. You want to spend time with him and don't want to admit it."

"Ahh, don't make me puke. Just for that, you get to sit through my lesson and work on your drawing. Don't get so affronted. You used to scribble pictures in the dirt. Now, get a pencil and one of those books with the empty pages and draw, girl, or my lessons end now."

"Oh, fine." She braced her hands against the table as she got up. "Don't expect anything I draw to end up anything recognizable."

Her friend left to find some supplies and Cate waited for them both to come back—so much for studying in secret and surprising him. She glanced over at the storage room where she hid the door, her thoughts drifting to the courtyard. A happy thrill went through her and made the coming lessons with Teddy endurable.

Later, they left Cate and made their way back to their rooms. Caden's neck and hands were stiff from use. Once she got over expecting miracles, she settled into enjoying the process of drawing. After a while of scribbling everything she saw in front of her, her brother gave her a basic art book he found. The lessons were easy with plenty of pictures for her to follow. Any time she got stuck, he explained the instructions. By the time she stopped for the day, her results had pleased her.

Things between Cate and her brother were not quite as smooth. He had the patience of a rock, and she had the temper of lava, so it made for a colourful afternoon. Still, despite the episodes of books, pencils, and words flying, Cate seemed to make an impressive amount of growth. She possessed a mind for remembering things and connecting dots.

They entered the sunroom as the people drifted away to go for supper. The gardens overflowed with flourishing plants and ripening vegetables. Hanna improved the lighting to some kind of bulb system their Pa discovered on a scrounge. Now, with the help of many hands, they found carrot seeds, onions, tomatoes, and even peppers, and the ever-present potatoes.

And by the grace of fate, they had the bees. Sahra Murray was a gnarly old lady who had been one of several who worked the bee farm that survived along with the chickens and a portion of the vegetable gardens the Upperlords tended for their food. It turned out that for years she cultivated her own hive in secret, making honey for her family and select friends. Plus, she incubated a bundle of little chicks and a few roosters too. When Mrs. Fish told her they were leaving Undercity, she snuck out her hives and birds and brought them along. At first, she was uncertain if the bees would survive the transition, but they revived and made their home amid the flowers. Everyone relaxed, knowing no bees meant no food unless they wanted to figure out how to hand pollinate. The birds roosted in one of the empty shops, and the roosters loved to crow at dawn, the sound echoing through the mall.

"Life is comfortable here, isn't it?"

He nodded. "It's certainly better than what we had."

"But you still wish for more."

Her brother shot her a doubtful glance. "I try to think this is it. Everyone happy here, everyone growing, learning and living, and stuff, but..."

"But there's always the chance we'll run out of food, water, whatever," she finished for him. "Yes. And there's the chance the Upperlords will find us. Though I don't understand why they'd want to."

"And there's always that," he agreed, waving his hand. "I guess they don't have a reason other than greed to search for us. It's that the fear is always in us. I know Henri doesn't want to waste his days sitting there listening for shifting rocks and pebbles."

"You're teaching him to read, aren't you," she asked with a sly glance.

A slight blush coloured his cheeks. "Yes, but you are not supposed to know."

"Why not?"

"Because, he realized you like it when I read to you and he's figured out you're not fond of gifts."

"Ugh," she said with an exaggerated grimace though the brute's gesture pleased her. "He should learn to read 'cause he wants to, not so he can read to me."

"He is learning because he wants to; he wants to so he can read to you," her brother said with an annoying grin.

"And again I say 'ugh'," she said and screwed up her face at him.

They went through the lobby and into the kitchen, spying Henri and Jolon standing in a corner helping themselves to some food. It was a steaming stew which made Caden's mouth water. "Mmmmm," she said, breathing in the wonderful vapours. "Yum." She took a bowl from the pile and spooned herself a large helping.

"Oh, man, that's a pleasant change from potatocakes and cookies," said Teddy and helped himself to his own serving.

Jolon slurped a spoonful as they walked toward a free table. "Weren't sure you two would show up on time," he said with juices dripping from his lips.

"The food isn't going anywhere. You could wait till you're at the table and eat there. More of it would stay in your mouth that way," Caden said, giving him a disgusted frown.

Her little brother made a face, but waited until they sat down to eat more. Caden tried not to be uncomfortable when Henri held her chair and sat down beside her. Teddy had a mischievous grin on, but kept his comments to himself.

"So, what happened today?" Teddy asked.

"It was pretty quiet," Jolon said between spoonfuls. "They suspect some rocks shifted."

"Yur Pa's thinkin' opening up and checkin'," Henri added.

"Georges figures that might be a good idea, but the others believe it might expose them to discovery. Hanna thinks they're all bonkers and wants to seal the passages up permanently, but Dorkas says if we do that, we'll have no way of getting back. Mr. and Mrs. Fish both want to send him back before sealing the tunnel, but they muttered that between them, so the suggestion is not on the list of choices. Too bad. I would help."

"Getting back, getting back where?" Caden asked. "Back to Undercity? Why would we want to do that?"

Teddy played with his food as though it didn't taste as good as before. "In case things fall apart here."

She regarded him with a puzzled gaze. "Why would things fall apart? And even if they did, nothing can be worse than life in Undercity. People have homes here, real homes with enough room for everyone."

"Nuf room to grow," Henri added with a gaze she refused to interpret.

"Who knows," said a voice behind her.

Caden smiled at her mother and father who joined them. They both appeared weary as though they had spent the day beating a cement wall. "Been arguing with the elders?" she asked, and they both nodded.

"I take it, it shows," Pa said as he sat down, an exhausted grin playing on his lips.

"Just a little around the eyes."

He chuckled and sighed as she patted his hand. "If those people ever sort themselves out, this would be a real paradise."

"Problem is, they need to agree, and there are too many agendas to do that," her father added, starting in on his food.

"What about Georges," Teddy asked. "What's she doing about all this?"

"Georges never wanted to be a leader; she said so from the start. She didn't care when they asked her not to use her Upperlord title, and she cares even less about being a part of the council. Georges' is happy things are better for people, but hates politics."

Ma's expression soured. "Georges is a sieve—holds nothing."

"Yes, but even sieves are useful." Pa wiggled an admonishing finger. "She has her moments. They are not impressive nor not often, but she does have them."

"So are you going to open the tunnels?" Teddy asked, pushing his bowl aside.

Their father shrugged. "It might be good to check on things. There might be people on the other side who still need our help. We left lots behind."

"Problem is, we might end up with the Upperlords that way and enough people on this side want to be in charge," Ma added. She stuffed a few strands of frizzed hair under a blue headband and sighed.

"I found some terrific supplies to start a proper school," Teddy said, in what Caden understood to be an attempt at a change of topic.

Their parents smiled at him. "This would be good," their mother said, patting his hand. "A little education might help people sort out their fears and such."

"I thought we might use one of the bigger rooms with all the tables. Caden's going to help the little ones with art projects and stuff, and I'm going to teach reading." He glanced at Jolon. "We need someone to help with math and sciences."

"So you said," he said with his habitual roll of the eyes. Their mother and father gave him an expectant look, and he caved. "Fine," he said, exhaling like a deflating balloon. "Though why you think I'm good at math confuses me."

"So you went scrounging?" Pa asked, his blue eyes lighting up.

"Just a little," Teddy admitted.

"They found a secret room filled with books," Deb said while she wandered up and crawled into her mother's lap.

"Where've you been, you little mouse?"

She yawned and snuggled her mother. "Mrs. Fish had us kids playin' games and weedin' plants. All tired."

"I'll get her some food," said Jolon after Ma eyed him.

"A room full of books, hey?" Pa said and Teddy flushed with guilt. "So my little gophers have been finding more treasures. Where is it?"

"Up these stairs, through this hall, and around these other stairs, through Cate's alcove, and down more stairs and halls, and such," Deb explained, weaving her hands about. "It's tiring to get to, but full of cats." She placed a hand on either side of her mother's face and peered into her eyes. "Can I keep Mr. Poufy?"

She gave a tolerant smile. "Who is Mr. Poufy?"

"Deb, didn't you ask Ma about the cat yet?"

The little girl put on her biggest innocent eyes. "I was going to yesterday, but then I thought you might 'cause you're bigger than me."

"Oh, sure. You pick the oddest times to get timid." Caden sighed and leaned back in her chair. "Mr. Poufy's a kitten Deb claimed as her own. I think it has taken up residence under my bed. The bookstore has lots of cats if anyone needs any."

Her parents traded glances. "It might be helpful."

"For?"

"Mice and such," her mother said though Caden suspected the 'such' involved cooking. "So, you found Cate?"

Caden nodded.

"You two haven't gotten together for quite a while. How is she?"

She shrugged. "Ah, she's always good and always fiercely independent."

"Yes, you know we wanted to take her in too when we found you," her mother said with a squeeze of Caden's arm.

The pressure of her mother's fingers was comforting. "Yeah, sometimes I wish she had accepted. She seems so lonely."

"Yes, but she has you."

Caden gave her a small smile. It was true but difficult. Her friend had so many defences she needed to tread carefully.

"You want more?" Henri asked, interrupting them by taking hold of her bowl. She shook her head, and he cleared the bowls.

Jolon came back with another serving for himself and gave Deb her food. Teddy and Pa left together to talk about the school and other things. Mrs. Fish showed up with her usual brood in tow. Ma moved her chair over, and they pulled up another table, filling their quiet corner with commotion.

Exhausted, Caden slipped away and went back to her room. Her head ached from all the noise and from all the concentrating she had done, but she was happy with her progress. She closed the door to her room and stretched out on her bed. Rain fell outside. Little patters of wet hit her window, lulling her to sleep.

Chapter 4

Cate stared out the glass door in the apartment. Rain splattered down and obscured her view. Her cat curled in a ball on the armchair and seemed rather content to wash its private parts, revealing his physical gender. Some time during the morning she decided to call the creature Sunny because he reminded her of sunlight. Would it be cruel to toss the animal outside to see if it was safe? Sunny paused mid-grooming lick and gave her a pout before turning around. She took the hint.

"Yeah, don't worry, I wasn't gonna do it," she said, but he ignored her.

She put her fingers on the handle and hesitated. The leaves seemed fine, but the flowers all curled up. Did the rain or the sun setting cause that?

Anxious, she sat on the chair beside the door and lit a candle on the side table. An ache throbbed through her head, and she rubbed her temples, realizing she hadn't eaten since earlier in the day. A search through her pockets yielded nothing. On impulse, she got up and slid the door open. The sound of raindrops drifted in. A long ledge hung above the entryway, which sheltered a few feet in front of her from the wet. Terrified and exhilarated, she stepped out. A touch of cool wind stirred up a perfumed and delicious air.

Wonderful. A pleased grin clung to her lips. With reluctance, she went back in, not quite ready to step into the rain, but content with venturing so far. She went to the kitchen and searched for something to eat. A few shelves held several tins and boxes though some showed chew marks and mouse droppings.

"Hey, you are sloppy in your duties," she told Sunny, but the creature yawned and flicked his tail.

Humming, she pulled out a couple of cans and wiped off the lids. They seemed good, not bloated or dented. After rummaging through the drawers, which were clean of mice trails, she found some cutlery, an opener, and several large spoons. She took out an opener and removed the lid of one of the cans.

"Bbbeeeeffff st... st... stew," she worked out with pride, remembering her lessons from earlier. Hopeful, she sniffed at the chunky goo, which smelled pretty good. She stuck a digit in and licked the juices. Not bad, kinda cold. Would be better if warmed up. A check under the counter produced a little pot on a stand and an assortment of candles the right size to fit underneath. Cate lit another candle and pushed the disk under the ceramic pot. After, she poured the soup in and left the food to warm.

Weary, she stretched out in a large chair, put up her feet. The place was comfortable and furnished with a couch, a chair, a few tables, and some things she never discovered before. One wall had books and other trinkets stuffed on shelves and metal boxes with odd buttons or knobby things. Most of the decor would make Upperlords drool if any were around. Even a few pleasant pictures of scenic places and carefree people hung on the walls. They all seemed so happy, smiling and standing outside amid the trees and flowers. A cool, perfumed breeze flowed in through the open door, refreshing her.

Sunny jumped into her lap, kneading her leg before curling up again, purring. Cate frowned with disapproval but scratched him behind the ears. The place wasn't bad. All it needed was a little work, and she would have a home all her own. The couch was comfortable though she suspected one of the doors down the short hall off the kitchen might be a bedroom. A separate room with a real bed sounded enticing. The cat protested as she deposited him on the floor. After taking a moment to stretch, she went to the first door, which opened to a small bathroom. A cursory check under the sink and in a thin closet by the toilet gave her towels, soaps, which might still be good, and a few other useful items. The taps proved useless as she suspected. They squeaked and clunked, but nothing happened.

She found little behind the next narrow door except a few crystallized bottles, a broom, and a mop sitting in a bucket. The cleaners could go, but the rest had value. After taking the pail out, she wiped the bottom clean and put it on the porch to collect rain. If nothing else, she could boil the water and wash up.

The last door led to a bedroom. Sunny rushed in before her and stirred up a flurry of creatures under the once blue and white covers which sat on the bed. Mice. She shuddered as he had a fantastic time crunching his supper. Cate left the cat and the mice. The couch was better, and she would check for any good clothing later.

With her stomach grumbling as the smell of cooking food drifted in, she went back to the kitchen. The stew wasn't burning hot but bubbled enough. She snatched a bowl out of a cupboard and filled it. After pulling a spoon from a drawer, she went back to the chair. Another couple of cats wandered in as she ate.

"Supper's that way," she said, pointing toward the bedroom with the spoon. The two kitties rushed past without so much as a purring thank you. That was fine. They could have the room. The bed was too infested to save, but the couch fit to her frame well.

All she needed to do was figure out a way to tell Caden and Teddy she found a new home without bringing them over. Or if all else failed, seal off the glass door enough, so they didn't know she went outside. Comfy and full, she pulled a blanket over herself and continued to enjoy the rain by candlelight. This was hers, all hers, at least for now.

The caress of something soft and cool made Caden open her eyes. Ma bent over her with a cloth to her forehead.

"Uhmmmuh, once more and again. I'm not so good today," she said, throat dry and head aching.

Her mother nodded. "Don't worry, love. I'm here. Any pain?"

"The usual."

"Well, now. A good day's rest and you'll be fine," Ma advised with a pat to her hand. "Cate's here to keep you company for a while."

Caden peered toward the chair by the window. Cate waved at her, a stack of books beside her. "Teddy suggested I bring you art books in case you're up to drawing."

"And until then, she gets to practice reading, and you get to listen," Deb wriggled into the chair beside Cate with a floppy book in her hand. "But we should cuddle up on my bed 'cause my stuffies want to listen too."

"Yeah, kid, we'll read to the stuffies too," Cate said with a slight grin. They got up and went over to the bed, crawling in among the lions, bears, puppies, monkeys, and kittens Deb stored on her bed.

"I'll leave you three to your books," Ma said with a smile. "I put some food by your bed. Snack now and I'll bring you something more later." After she left, Caden munched a few crackers.

"You stink," Deb said, making a face and pushing Cate away.

"Hey, kid," objected Cate.

"The shower is that way," the little girl said, pointing to the bathroom. "Works too and feels good. I like the bubbles."

Cate frowned at her and turned to Caden for help. She grinned. "Use some of my clothes. They're in the first drawer."

Her friend pulled at her shirt. "Are you saying I stink too?"

"Well," she said with a sly wink to Deb. "You're not peeling paint yet, but your clothes might stand by themselves."

"Just for that, I should make you two suffer."

"Remember, I'm sick," said Caden, taking on a mock sad face.

Cate heaved an exaggerated sigh. "Fine, but you better have good stuff, or I'm wearing what I got." She pulled open the drawer and rummaged through Caden's stuff.

"Not a lot of clothes inside, a few short-sleeved shirts and cotton pants, but they are clean and in good shape. Some new undergarments too," she said. "All my clothes are too baggy or too short, so some things should fit you better."

Her friend took some clothes out and whirled around, her curls whipping around her head. "The things I do for you people."

"Don't worry, you won't dissolve," Deb said in a perfect imitation of their mother.

Caden laughed though the movement hurt her head. She shut her eyes and felt the weight of Deb on the bed. She peeked at her sister who snuggled in beside her.

"I'll read until she comes back," Deb said, plumping a pillow behind her head. She opened a pretty book with two little bear children playing a game on the first page.

As she closed her eyes again, she listened as Deb's tale. The story was simple, but her sister read well, using sound effects and drama to her fullest abilities.

A knock sounded, and Deb scurried to the door.

"Hello, Teddy," she said, opening the door wide and skipping back to the bed. "I'm reading and doing good too. Right, Cadie?"

"I guess, sure," she said and waved a hand at her brother. "Hey."

He smiled and glanced about the room as though expecting to find someone else. "Hey, how you doing?"

"Alive," she replied. "She's in the bathroom having a shower."

"Huh? Who?" he asked, rubbing at his head.

"You know who."

"We made her take a shower," Deb explained, planting herself in her pile of animals. "Cate's supposed to read with me, but she was stinky." She wrinkled her nose and fluffed a bunny.

Teddy grinned. "I'll bet she took that real well."

"She took it fine," Cate said, coming back in the room, patting her neck with a towel. Her long hair fell in curling ribbons around her. She had put on one of Caden's blue shirts, which made her blue eye brighter.

Caden's brother made a low noise in his throat and dropped his gaze to the floor, his cheeks tinting pink. "Hey."

"Hey, yourself," she said, sinking to the edge of Deb's bed. "What are you doing here? You run out of books?"

"No, why would I... what?" He stumbled over his words, confused.

They laughed, and he grimaced.

"Don't worry, Ted, she's only trying to keep me smiling," Caden said and patted the bed. "Sit down."

"Ah, I would, but I came here for a reason. I mean, I wanted to see how you were doing, but I also needed to talk to Cate."

"Well, I'm doing okay. Just tired, and Cate is right here so talk away," she said, wondering what he had to say.

"Hey, Deb, can you go to the kitchen and get more crackers for Caden?" he asked, and their little sister made a face.

"Why me? I'm comfy."

"Go on," Cate ordered, "I'll fill you in later."

She grumbled and tossed her stuffed animals aside. "Fine, but you better tell me everything."

"Deal."

"Okay, so what's pulling at you?" Caden asked after Deb left.

Her brother sat in a chair by the window, his face serious. "I thought of something."

Caden raised an eyebrow. "We figured that."

"There's been some trouble. Everyone's tied up in knots, and they're starting to fight among themselves. Dorkas is spreading rumours that the Upperlords are coming, and others are saying we're almost out of meat."

"Well, Dorkas is a twit and what difference does it make if we have meat? We still have stuff to eat," Cate asked.

"People need protein."

They stared at him. "And protein is..." Caden asked.

"I don't understand the technical parts, but we need protein, which is mostly found in meat. It makes our muscles work or something like that. Point is, we need meat, and we don't have meat. The few chickens we brought have stopped laying eggs. Ma's contemplating harvesting the cats we found. Given there is an abundance of them, it doesn't sound like a bad idea, but some people don't want to eat cat."

Cate made a face. "Don't blame them."

"So, what's your idea," Caden asked, choosing to ignore the thought of eating cat. If she had to, she had to. For now, her stomach was having enough difficulties.

"I want to sneak back to the other side," he confessed, gazing steadily at both of them.

"The other side as in Undercity," Cate said, her one eye wide.

"Yep," he said, nodding.

Caden sank back into her pillow, mouth dry. "To achieve what?"

"Get more chickens?" Cate offered with a wry expression.

He gave a small shrug. "Perhaps. Mostly I want answers. I want to find out if they are searching for us. I want to know what they are doing. If we could answer some of the questions and stories, which are getting people all riled, we might settle into dealing with more important matters."

"So, you want me to go with you," Cate said after a moment's silence.

"This is a reckless idea," Caden said, frowning. "How are you even going to get back to the warehouse?"

"Yeah, this is foolish."

"And you want me to go with you."

"Yes, I want you to go with me."

She rolled her eye, and he shook his head. "Believe me, you are not my first choice."

"Oh, thanks."

"Caden can't and Jolon is too..."

"Bulky?" Cate offered, and he frowned.

"Young. He's too young and unmotivated."

"What about Henri?" Caden asked, knowing her friend's disdain for helping.

"Henri is too obvious. I don't want anyone to know what we're doing. If he disappears, Pa and Ma will know..."

"You're up to no good," Caden chuckled.

He nodded. "Something like that."

"So, me it is," Cate said, donning a mischievous grin. She nudged him with her foot. "This might be fun."

Before he could reply, Deb came in with Henri carrying a tray behind her. She bounded over to her bed while Henri put the tray on the bedside table. He wiped his hands on his pants and grinned at her.

"I brought food. Ma busy."

"Thanks," she mumbled, and he waved toward the bed.

"Child said you tired today. Child said she reading to you. Would like to help."

Her sister smiled like she won a war. "Thought you might like that."

Caden threw her a dirty expression.

Teddy motioned to Cate. "We gotta go."

She got off the bed and tossed a book to Henri. "Enjoy. She gets grumpy when you stop."

+

"So, how are we going to get to the other side?" Cate asked, keeping up with Teddy's stride. They hurried through the fountain plaza and past the sunshine room.

"I found some maps. I'm thinking if we trace some of the pathways; we might find a way back. I'd rather not sneak in the way we got here if we can."

She followed him inside a room full of equipment, bags, and other odd bunches of stuff. "You ever thought of searching the vent system? They seem to weave everywhere."

"Not always safe," he said while rifling through an assortment of papers. He pulled one out and unfolded it, spreading the map on an empty table. "They can open up almost anywhere at any time. You can fall into a hole or water, or even outside."

"Is outside so bad?"

He squinted up at her, shrugging. "Don't know about now, but at the beginning some pretty bad stuff happened, I guess. That's what the stories say."

She studied her skin, which seemed normal, perhaps darker since the day before. Was that a problem? The morning came with warmth and golden sunshine, so she spent quite a while in the courtyard. She could still feel the intensity of the rays on her face. "But it seems so beautiful outside."

"Yeah, it does. One day I think someone will step outside."

"Why don't they?"

"I think they are waiting for signs of life, an animal or birds to show the air is good and they are not going to roast." He went back to studying his map, running his finger along a blue line. "This is us here," he said, tapping a large star. "Uppercity is over here." He tapped another star halfway across the map. "This is the walkway we took to get from one to the other." She watched his finger run along another blue line.

"So, what's this?" she asked, pointing to a yellow line which, ran to the left of Teddy's line.

"Good question. According to the legend at the bottom, it is a service walkway or delivery route. This could be our way in."

"Guess we won't know until we try. If it's intact, we're golden."

He kept a steady gaze with her. "And if it's not, we could be dead."

He had such clear eyes, two orbs, bright and expressive. She felt a strong temptation to either poke one or kiss it. "Dead's fine too. At least, we would die trying as opposed to sitting in a corner waiting for starvation to come."

"Right," he said with a grimace. "That's one way to approach the situation." He pulled out a stash from a pile and tossed the grey pack to her. "We'll need some supplies. I took water and food from the kitchen, so we only need the air tanks and lights."

"You were pretty certain I'd come with you, were you?" she asked, raising her eyebrow at him.

He flushed a little around the ears. "I figured you would, yeah."

"Why?"

"Because you're like me, you don't like sitting still."

She thought about this for a moment before nodding. "Guess you're smarter than you look."

"And I guess you're nicer than you seem," he retorted, and she punched him in the arm.

"Don't bet on it."

They walked out of the storeroom and across the sunroom as though it was a normal day. Nobody paid them much attention. After slipping down a few halls, they came to a back doorway. Teddy glanced at her, one eyebrow raised. She shrugged and shoved the door open.

"Proper scrounging protocol is to don an oxygen mask before opening a door," he said with a disapproving twitch of his eyebrows.

Cate pulled out her handlight. "Yeah, and I also know those who don't care already checked this area. Your family is not the only scroungers from Undercity. Around here others discovered places you and yours never thought to search."

"You've been this way?" he asked, stepping through the entrance.

She passed him and went down the hall, the beam of her light sweeping back and forth. "Nope, but Murky has, and Dweep, a few others too. They said there's not much down here—just halls and doors. I think Dweep lives in a store a couple of stalls from here. He's a little unstable, so we leave him to his space. Thinks he's the king of mice. Doesn't eat them. Murky does, so they're bitter enemies, but Dweep keeps them as pets. Always has one in his hair." She shuttered. "Can't stand those tiny paws and teeth."

"I remember Murky, but I don't think I've met Dweep."

"No doubt. He doesn't trust people, only mice."

He chuckled, and she grinned.

"So, according to our map, we keep going until we find two double doors to our left. These should lead us through to another hallway and a staircase," he told her, juggling his light and his map as they walked.

"Fun. Always stairs no matter where you go. Our ancestors were in good shape."

"Apparently not," he said, tucking his map into his pack. "As far as I have read, they took elevators or moving stairs, and then bought gym memberships."

"What's a gym membership?"

"Something you buy with the intent of getting into shape, and then you don't go to," he clarified with a laugh. "I don't know. There's so much we've lost..."

"Some doesn't sound much like it's worth finding again," she said with a snort.

"Yeah, it does seem like it sometimes, but many things, like medicine and stuff, would be fantastic to rediscover."

They came to the double doors he had mentioned, and he stopped. "Mask," he said as he pulled his out.

She scrunched her nose in distaste but took hers out. "Yuck, these things stink."

He grinned through the plastic. "Yep," he said, his voice distorted.

They pushed on the door together. The path was a mess of crumbled walls and trash with a couple of extra hallways and a crumbling staircase. She looked to Teddy while pointing to her respirator. He glanced at his meter and nodded. Amused, she chuckled and removed her mask.

"Hey, it's important to be safe," he said though a little color crept up his neck.

"Sure," she said and turned her light away from him. Footprints scuffed the dirt of a passage leading in another direction. "Looks like Murk and Dweep have gone further than I thought."

Teddy glanced down the hall. "Doubt it goes anywhere helpful."

"So, I guess we've got some climbing to do." She stuck her handlight under one arm and began to crawl over the rubble. "The air is kind of dank, though."

"Yeah, some pipes burst or something. Most dry out after a while, but a few still trickle stuff. Nuna figures they filter rainwater down from the roof."

"Which means there's air coming in from outside too," she said, pausing on a crumbled wall to pull out her water flask and take a drink.

He shrugged a shoulder and sat across from her, taking out his water. "I guess that's the logical conclusion."

"So, the air is breathable."

"That's a possibility too, I suppose. Then again, it's hard to tell."

"For a guy who found paradise, you're awfully pessimistic," she said as she rose and went forward again.

"Just a little nervous about the whole outside thing," he admitted as he followed her.

"Do you want to go outside?" she asked, keeping her eye on the path as holding a handlight while crawling through the debris wasn't easy. She thought about the morning in the little garden, wondering if she could bring him there. Perhaps, if he proved trustworthy. So far she wasn't sure. Still, he was pleasant to talk to when he wasn't a twit.

"Sometimes I do, and sometimes I don't," he admitted. "It does seem beautiful beyond the wall, and I always wanted to let the rain soak my skin, but..."

"It's so open and unsheltered."

"You like to finish my sentences, don't you?" he said with a friendly chuckle. "Yes, or, at least, that's all I've seen. You ever wonder if we are the only people around? The books describe whole continents existing with people, cities and populations before the disaster. Is anyone else still alive in other places? Did disaster hit everywhere and if not why hasn't anyone come to help here?"

"Wasn't the air toxic after?" she asked, her foot slipping on a rock. She grunted and readjusted her step.

"Supposedly. Yeah, that's what they say," he said, halting to pull out his map. "Doesn't mean we're the only ones who survived. Some of the domes in other countries might have held. There might be whole cities somewhere filled with people living their lives with room to grow and food to eat."

"You can't be satisfied with the little paradise here, can you?"

"Not when there's more to explore." He pointed toward another set of doors hanging half off the hinges. "This is our next exit."

"You sure we shouldn't put the masks on?" she asked, arching an eyebrow.

He made a face. "So funny. I think we're okay."

They helped each other make their way through the doors. Cate dropped her handlight and had to reach through bits of cement to get it back. She scraped her arm and took a deep breath.

"Ah, fun," she said, coughing as they disturbed the dust.

"You okay?" he asked, helping her up.

"Yep. Tough as a rock."

"Inside and out," he said, and she almost didn't hear him.

Was that the way he saw her, hard? He was right to a degree. It was painful to be soft when life was so hard.

"Okay, so this isn't good," she said, dusting herself off as she found a place to stand. She turned her light toward the mess that was once a staircase. "I suppose this is climbable in some sense, but it's not going to be pretty."

He tugged on a metal railing, pulling harder and harder to check how stable it was, and the rail held.

She arched her eyebrows. "That doesn't prove anything."

"No," he said as he hoisted his body upward. "But, sometimes there's no other way to tell except to go up."

"Sure, that makes sense. And when we go tumbling down, we'll know what a bad idea this is," she said, following him.

She had shoved her flashlight into the side pocket of her pack, so the light shone upward and let her hands free to climb. The metal was cold and bit into her skin. She twisted about until her feet were under her, putting them between the rails. The support wobbled, and she cursed Teddy to release tension.

"Yes, it's a dumb idea," he said back down to her. "But I couldn't think of another."

Strands of hair dropped into her face; she spat a clump out, wishing she had tied it back or cut the mess off. "Yeah, well, we might take more time and consider our options."

"Careful of that rung, it's a little loose," he cautioned, pointing at it with his boot.

She swung to the left, tightening her muscles. Her limited vision was terrible, and her pack dug into her back. "How much farther?"

He stopped and propped himself between the wall and the railing. Reaching behind him, he took out a light and shone it upward. The banister went up about ten feet further before connecting with a partial stair. "Do you think it's stable?"

"Hope so, or we're mushed potatoes," she said, and he laughed.

"Yeah."

By the time they reached the stair, her arms shook with the effort. She swung herself up and sat on a filthy step, breathing heavy as she slung off her stash. The sound of the metal buckles hitting the cement echoed through the stairwell.

"Gotta eat something," she told him as Teddy sat down beside her and took off his stash. She pulled out some potatocakes and handed him one. "The one thing I hope is one day I will never need to eat another one of these again."

"That's what Jolon always says," he said, taking a bite.

She laughed. "Geez. Even he's tired of them. That's bad." She took a large bite, the food dry in her mouth. A large swig of water helped her chew enough to make her stomach stop grumbling. "They're not so bad, I suppose. They satisfy."

"Yes, they do," Teddy agreed and rubbed his hands over his face. "Oh, damn, I thought I was done doing this."

She smacked him in the leg. "You sound like you're ancient. I'm calling you old guy from now on. Besides, I recognized the gleam in your eyes; you love this."

"All right, fine. I love exploring and learning, but this danger stuff is wearing."

Cate snatched up her stash and put it back on, securing her light in the top. "That's better. Come on, old guy, let's get moving."

"Fine," he said and got up. "I'm coming."

The staircase widened and got more stable as they went, though pieces of drywall, chunks of wood, bits of metal, and dirt made the climbing difficult.

"How much farther to go?" she asked, stopping to clean out a rock from her shoe.

"Can't say. I'm searching for a door that opens," he said, passing her.

She caught up with him and kept pace. For a while, all they did was step and step. They passed a couple of doors, but they wouldn't budge, so they went on.

"You know something," Teddy said as they went.

"We're going up?"

"Ha, yeah, and we're getting along too. Caden would be amazed."

"We can get along," she said, her legs tired. "All it takes is for you to not be so superior."

"I'm not superior. You just misunderstand me."

"Oh? I'm that blockheaded, huh?"

He took on an exasperated expression. "Yeah, you're doing it right now. That's not what I meant. You decided what my words meant without finding out if that's what I intended them to mean."

"You mean that, don't you?" she said, unable to resist.

"Ha, ha," he said and yelped as the rail gave way.

She caught him by the stash though his weight slammed her into the lower part of the rail. His handlight fell and spun down the stairwell. They stayed still for a moment, him dangling half over the edge and her straining to keep him with her.

"Don't move," she gasped. "My grip's not so good."

"Neither's mine," he grunted, the fingers of his left hand barely curling around the stub of iron left attached to the cement.

She fell in an awkward position with her legs twisted, so most of her weight was on her arms, making it hard to readjust her grip. Carefully, she wedged her left foot around the bar where bolts held the rail to the step below. "Okay, I'm going to hook my right leg through the rails. As long as this section holds, I should be able to get a better grip and pull you up."

"That would be appreciated," he panted.

It was difficult to see him as her light skimmed the top of his hand.

Cate took a deep breath and bent her leg around an iron bar. The step under her pressed into her ribs, but she couldn't shift without losing him. She twisted her left arm out and grabbed hold of the strap to his stash, which gave her the freedom to improve the hold of her right hand. With one tremendous twist of her upper body, she yelled and yanked him up to where he could find more leverage. They both pulled again, and he was safe, half on her, but safe.

"Get off," she huffed, patting him on the head, his face too close. "You're too heavy."

He smiled, his eyes wide and shining. "Thanks," he mumbled and did as she asked.

She took a moment to catch her breath before she sat up. It shouldn't feel so good to be near him. It was irritating and unfair. He was as perfect as a person got in their world and she hated perfect; it was untrustworthy, unsafe.

"Come on," she said, thwacking him on the leg. "Let's get off this thing before it gives way on both of us."

"Good idea," he grinned and got up, staying as close to the wall as possible. "You lead, I lost my light."

She nodded and went in front of him, hugging the wall as he did to be safe. As she reached more solid ground, she shone her handlight in front of her. She discerned another landing up ahead. The door appeared to be partially open. They arrived in moments and squeezed through.

"You realize we have to go back down that way," she said, and he frowned at her.

"Why? Why did you say that? I was enjoying the moment of relief at being on solid ground. Now all I can think is we have to go back."

"That's what I'm here for, to keep you alert and thinking," she told him with a grin. She swept the area in front of them with the handlight. The hall ended in a gigantic mound of busted pipes, wood, and fragmented stone. "Then again, we might need to keep going up."

He made a face and held out a hand. "Give me the light for a moment," he said, and she passed it over. As he leaned back, he poked his head out the door, shining the light upward. "Option one, going up. Not much use. It all ends in one more section, and there is no landing anymore," he said as he turned back to her. He searched the room with her light. The walls were bare cement with peeling yellow paint, and ceiling tiles hung from above. Their eyes met.

"Up?" he said.

"Up," she sighed.

Chapter 5

He stuck her light back in the side pocket of her stash the beam shining upward. "If we climb on some of this rubble we can hoist ourselves up."

"Yeah, 'cause I hauled your ass once today. Not interested in doing it again," she said as she searched for a good place to step.

For a scrawny guy, he was strong enough, she determined while he disappeared into the ceiling. He stuck a hand toward her.

"Come on, this isn't too bad as far as I can tell. There's a ledge to crawl along."

Cate climbed to him and grasped his hand. "Ahuhg, all this hoisting and heaving can't be good for the arms," she huffed, wriggling up beside him. "In fact, I'm pretty certain if I do much more, they're gonna pop right out of my body."

He chuckled and took the light from her pack, inching down the tiny smidge of an edge. "I thought you were all steel and iron."

She followed, his feet sticking inches from her face. "Ah, yes, I give that impression, but I'm afraid that's only in will. The rest of me is soft."

He snickered at this and for some reason, she blushed. Thankfully, he was in front, because she had no explanation for her embarrassment.

"So, how do we know this is the right way?" she asked, focusing on the task.

"Good question. As far as I can tell from the map, this should head toward the warehouse."

Cate worked her neck to relieve the tension building in the muscles. "As far as you can tell. Hmmm, not comforting. In fact, as a leader and guide, you're sucking at the moment."

"I'm going to believe you're talking to ease your fears. Otherwise, I might get offended and tell you to go flog yourself."

"Flog, flog? Doesn't that require other people to be achieved?"

"Are you asking for my help?"

She coughed, dust gathering in her throat. "Funny. And here I thought I might almost like you."

"Almost like me," he repeated before sneezing several times. "I suppose like is better than almost hating me."

Dirt stirred up as they moved and the particles decided her breathing passages made the best place to make a new home. "That's the best you're gonna get for now. Tell you what. Get us out of this and I'll think about changing your status."

"Deal." His foot jerked back as he coughed.

Instinctively, she moved, and went the wrong way as everything buckled under her, sending her tumbling downward.

"Cate!"

She lay still, the breath knocked out of her. Wheezing, she worked air back into her lungs.

"Cate," he repeated, shining the light down.

Drained, she waved a couple of fingers at him and groaned. The surface of whatever she fell on crunched and collapsed under her weight. Her body seemed to be still intact, but she held still in case any limbs fell off.

He jumped down beside her and leaned close, his concern evident. "Anything broken? Say something."

"Get the damn light out of my eye," she gasped and swatted at the handlight as she sat up.

"Well, at least, you landed on a bunch of boxes. Might have been worse." He brushed hair from his face and took off his stash.

Worse, yeah, her aching body disagreed. She ran her tongue over dry lips and pulled off her stash. After sipping a long drink from her bottle, she stretched with care, checking for anything broken.

"So, what is this, another storage room?" she asked, flicking strands of hair from her face.

"Seems to be," he said. "We should rest here for a while. Make sure you're okay and get our bearings."

She pulled at a box, knocking the cardboard flap back. Cracked plastic purses in a multitude of colours sat inside. She whispered a tiny thanks that the contents were not glass or rocks. "What did they do with all this stuff?"

"Good question," he said, pulling out the map. "Guess they needed more stuff because they had more people."

"How many?"

He shrugged. "Not too sure, but this city's population alone reached over a million before everything fell apart."

"That's scary," she said, trying to picture so many people. "With so many people, we can't be the only ones to survive."

"Mmmm, you would think. I don't like to dwell on past population levels. So many people dead is frightening to imagine."

Cate stood and worked the kinks out of her legs. The bruises would show up everywhere by morning. "Hey, you find where we are yet?"

He flipped the map over, biting on his lower lip. Cute quirk or annoying habit, she couldn't decide.

"No idea," he said, shaking his head. "We might be on the fourth floor of the north section of the mall, or in a completely different mall. This mess of buildings all join and spread out over blocks with all sorts of tunnels and passages. And that's not taking into account all the alterations since the devastation."

She peered over his shoulder. He was right. The map was a colourful spider's web except not as well structured. "You had us all sorted out when we started. Where did we go wrong?"

"Good question. As far as I can tell we should have gotten off on the second floor and turn to the left. Seems we ended up getting off on the third or fourth floor and turning right. Though it was a little hard to tell from the ceiling."

"So, what now?" she asked, sitting down on a box.

"I guess we start with figuring out a way out of this storage room that doesn't involve crawling through the ceiling."

"Agreed." She went to the door and knocked. "Where do you suppose this goes?"

Teddy pointed his hand light her way. "To the central part of the store would be the obvious guess."

A mischievous grin spread on her lips. "Shall we check it out? I'll even put a mask on."

"Why not? It's better than trying to read this dismal excuse for a guide," he said and tossed his map aside. He dug into his stash and pulled out his respirator.

She did likewise, giving him a thumb's up when she was ready. He passed over the light and turned the handle, cracking the door open an inch. Sunlight poured in, causing a moment of blindness. Cate blinked until her eye adjusted and gasped at the sight in front of her.

Outside, they were outside. The store was a burned out hull exposing them to the rest of the world. A strong gust of wind blew in. Teddy slammed the door. Stunned, he stood for a moment before turning toward her, all pale and blinking.

She didn't know what to say. He seemed so exhilarated and terrified simultaneously. The door only opened for a moment, yet he was shaking. Hands trembling, he pulled out his meter and checked the gauge before pulling the moulded plastic a few inches away from his face and sniffing. "We're safe," he said and swallowed hard. "I think. Yes?"

"Seems so," she said, taking off her mask. "Guess we can't go that way."

He stepped toward the door then backed away. "Yeah, no, we can't. No. We can't."

"Sit down, old guy, you're falling to pieces. It's not so bad. It was a moment, a second."

He crumpled down on a box, blinking as though trying to slow down his thoughts with his sweeping lashes. She put a hand to the door, longing to experience the wind again. Outside had become an addiction; a craving since the first time a small breeze touched her through the glass door. Now, her skin yearned for the caress.

"It was pleasant."

Teddy leaped to his feet. "Come on. No point sitting here."

She stared at him, caught between hope and bewilderment. "Outside?"

"No," he said, pointing the flashlight toward the back wall. "We might find another door over behind those boxes." He donned his mask. "Must lead back into the building. That's our best bet." Without another word, he strapped the light to his stash before dragging boxes aside.

Cate frowned but decided not to argue. Reluctantly, she put her mask and stash back on and helped clear a way to the back wall. After moving aside several boxes, they uncovered an exit.

"Okay, so here we go," she muttered through the plastic stuck to her face though she doubted he heard. She clutched the knob and pulled. It was stuck. She braced her leg against the wall and heaved with both hands. The door creaked, but only moved an inch. Teddy came in behind and put his arms around her, grasping the handle. Her first instinct was to elbow his ribs, but she stopped herself. He was only interested in opening the door, not her. Together, they tugged, straining before the door gave way, thrusting them backward into some boxes.

"Well," she gasped, trying to get up. "Fun."

He cleared her hair out of his face and fixed his respirator. "If you say so," he moaned as he helped her get up. "I think you bruised a rib."

"Aw, you're tougher than a little squishing from me," she said and gave him a hand up. They turned back toward the door, which gaped at them like it was innocent of any wrongs. She waved toward the opening. "After you, oh guy with the light."

As they went forward, Teddy analyzed the air with his meter. He gave a thumb up while removing his mask. After pausing to put his equipment away, he moved the light to his hand.

"Is this always necessary?" she asked as she took off the respirator.

"Used to be," he said as they went into the passage, which was much like every other hall they went through: dirty, cluttered, and dark. "Once, almost every tunnel a person went through held bad air. Many scroungers died at first until they found the air tanks. I think it was Pa's pa who dug them out of some shop with this big pool and ugly suits made of rubber. The place had lots of good tools. They had other tanks for oxygen too, bigger ones, but they were heavy to carry around and made manoeuvring difficult. My Pa said his pa said they were for deep sea diving."

She tilted her head, shrugging.

"That's when you go deep into the water, lets you breathe and stay down under the surface for long periods of time. They had these little tanks to teach smaller children in the pools, or that's what his pa said."

"What a strange world. I try to picture the past sometimes, and it just seems too much to see."

"Yep."

They walked on in silence for a moment, their footsteps echoing down the cement tunnel. Cate's thoughts dwelt on her outdoor experiences. The air seemed good. She seemed fine as far as she could tell. Everything about her was as healthy as ever. Her skin did seem a bit darker, but that didn't mean much. Still, maybe she was missing something. Perhaps she was contaminated and dying without even realizing it.

"Have you ever thought that the air inside is better because the air outside is good?"

"Might be," he said without looking back at her. "It's hard to say."

"The air seemed all good when we opened that door," she went on, a bit worried. "We didn't die or anything. We're not breaking out in spots even."

He stopped, turning toward her. Dirt and sweat streaked his face, and a shadow of concern lurked in his eyes. "We were unprotected for a moment, and we had the oxygen masks on. We're lucky. Who knows what prolonged exposure would do? Any venturing outside is not something anyone can do without planning. We can't just walk out."

"Why not?"

Teddy rubbed at his face. "Because," he paused, clenching his jaw as though he didn't know what to add to that, "it's just reckless."

"Kinda like this is, huh?" she said, gesturing to their surroundings.

"This is different. We know this, scrounging, digging in the rubble and wreckage... outside is all unknown."

She scowled, unsatisfied. "You're just scared."

That got him. His eyes flashed, and he strode off. "You think that if you want. I don't care. If you're so daring, go out. Go on. The door is back that way."

His reaction almost made her laugh. He was scared, but she didn't blame him. Terror nearly incapacitated her the first time she stood in a room with an open window. Her nerves still tingled every time she stepped into the courtyard. Still, he didn't have to be a jerk.

"That's real kind, thanks, a lot. Good to know you care."

He didn't say anything, and she didn't want him to. It was a bad idea to start liking him. They went on in silence, getting nowhere as far as she could tell. Fatigue pulled at her, throat dry and eye burning. Sweat trickled down between her shoulder blades from the heat.

"As fun as this is to just walk and walk and walk, I am tired. So, I'm sitting. If you want to continue, go ahead. This is turning out to be a pathetic waste of time."

Muscles throbbing, she slung her pack to the ground. After scraping a spot clean near the wall, she sunk down and leaned against the cement.

He continued for a few more steps, taking the light with him. Finally, he stopped and turned back.

"Fine, yeah, right. Of course, this is ridiculous," he muttered, slapping a hand against his leg. He came back and sat across from her, dropping his stash to the floor. "I didn't mean to... it's not that...."

"Are you trying to say something?" she asked, raising an eyebrow at him.

"Sorry," he mumbled, staring at the light in his hands.

"It's okay. I don't expect you to care about me. I wasn't the best choice as a companion on this journey. I was the only choice. You owe me nothing, and I owe you nothing."

He stared, the light distorting his features. "It's not like that. I...." He turned his gaze, lips a grim line. "Yes, I'm scared. Haa, ah, I'm terrified because I want it so much. I want to walk out of here and never come back. Every day, I have read books on the beauty that was the world: the space and the creatures, the vast, amazing diversity of everything. But I don't want to just read about waters so deep you need tanks of air to reach the bottom. I want to dive into those waters, immerse myself in a new world. I want to stand in a storm, not just see water fall against the glass isolating me from everything. I want, I want...." He paused, closing his eyes and leaning his head against the wall. "I want so much."

Cate frowned and glanced at the ground, understanding his desires. So much existed beyond their cement prison, enough space for everyone. Still, she refused to share anything about her journey outside. Terrified of losing her special moment, she let his declaration slide.

"You use a lot of big words, you know that?" she said, trying to lighten the mood.

Teddy chuckled. "Yeah. That's one thing I possess in limitless supply, words."

"Mmmm," she said with a grin as she shut her eye which burned. The air was so stale, so dead it gave her a headache now. Never used to. At least, she never noticed before. Now, she couldn't fully breathe no matter where she was.

"You hear that?"

She glanced toward him. He was sitting up, attentive. "What?"

"Listen."

It took a moment, but her ears perked and she straightened up—banging... talking? Whatever it was, the sound was constant now and not too far away. They both got off the floor.

"Okay, so we must be close," she said, lowering her voice.

"Yeah," he said in similar hushed tones. He leaned against the wall and put his ear against the drywall. "Can't hear much, but I think it's coming from that direction."

"Which is good because there doesn't seem to be much left of anything in the other direction," she said just to have something to say. The thought of reaching Uppercity made her nervous and uncomfortable.

He stepped away and peered up at the ceiling. "Seems like the voices are coming from up above us," he said, pointing to a vent above their heads.

"Of course, they are," she muttered, dreading the task of squirming through the ductwork. "It will be a hell of a job keeping quiet moving in there. How are we even going to get inside?"

They hunted for something to stand on but didn't find too much, mostly piles of dirt, decaying paper, and fallen ceiling tiles.

"There," he said, shining his light down the passageway. He rushed toward the blob of an object.

She followed and found him examining a broken tub with wheels that held plastic bags of plastic and paper. "Hey, I've seen these before in a few tunnels. Never could figure out why people put bags of bags in them. Handy for hauling though if you can find one in good condition."

This one was missing two wheels in the back, and a large crack spread down the middle.

Teddy lifted the cart and dumped the contents out. "Well, this seems solid enough to take our weight."

"As long as the crack doesn't spread, I guess, yeah," she said and helped pull it back to their access point. They were making too much noise, and she hoped that those on the other side wouldn't hear them.

With little effort, they tipped the plastic bin over and placed it under the vent. Height wise, it made reaching the opening easy, but there was still a fair way to climb.

"Guess we'll have to drag our packs behind us. You help me up, and I'll help you?" she said, giving him an optimistic grin.

He took the handlight and tied some string from his stash around one end. The other end, he tied to his shoe. After, he wedged the light into a hole, which once held one of the wheels. The beam shone toward the ceiling. "Sounds like a plan as long as this thing holds both of us," he said, nodding.

Cate got up first, holding her breath as she stabilized herself on the curved underside of the cart. He scrambled up beside her, the hefty plastic bin cracking and groaning under the added weight. They held each other's arms, waiting. She snickered, and he grinned as the support settled.

"Okay, up we go?" she said, and he bent a knee. With a tight hold on his hands, she stepped up, and he grunted. "Hey, I'm not so heavy."

"It's not that. My other leg is digging into some plastic ridge. You could be a feather, and this would still hurt."

She let go of one of his hands and grabbed the crown of his head. "Jeeze, you've got soft hair. Mine is like wire."

"I bath."

"Ha, ha. I bathed this morning if you remember. So stuff yourself," she said, grabbing the grated cover and pulling. It gave way, and so did her balance. She fell backward, hitting the ground hard.

"Hey, you okay?" he asked, rushing to her. He pulled the light out of the bin and shone it on her. "I tried to catch you, but...."

"I'm good," she snapped, her backside hurting. One eye wasn't a problem unless it came to balance and depth perception. "Adds another bruise." She took his hand and got up. "Let's keep going before I give up on this whole thing."

"I should have gone...."

"If you say you should have gone first, I'll smack you. I'm not made of glass. I should have been more careful. That's all. Besides, I'm tired of your hurt-puppy expression. Let's go," she growled and got back up on the tub.

He stuck the light back into place and climbed up before bending a knee for her again. She caught his hands and hoisted herself upward. Muscles straining, she wobbled as she grasped the ledge. "Hey, careful where you're grabbing," she said as he put a hand on her thigh to steady her.

"I am," he said, a tinge of embarrassment in his voice. "I mean, I'm being careful, not... just climb, would you?"

She laughed and took hold of the opening with her other hand. He pushed upward as she pulled and snaked into the vent. The place was so dry, her nasal passages hurt. It took a bit to twist around, but she wriggled back to where she could look down at him.

"You still there?" she called down, trying to see him. "You're in my blind spot."

"Sorry, here's your stash," he said, and he moved a little, holding up her pack.

"Ah, okay." After wedging her feet securely against the sides of the vent, she hauled her supplies up and shoved them behind her. "Okay, you're next," she said after taking his pack. "Well, come on, reach for me."

He made a little hop and grasped her hands.

"Oh, man. You're a weight and a half, aren't' you? If I'da known I was going to drag your sorry backside all day, I might have found something better to do."

"Funny again," he muttered and caught the edge. She grabbed his shirt and pulled while he thrust himself up. As he wrestled his way in, she backed up.

"And here we are stuck in a tunnel," she said as she squirmed around.

He came in by her, untying the light from the string attached to his foot.

"Clever idea."

Teddy grinned. "Thanks, I have one once in a while." He scanned the tunnel in front of them. "Though I'm not sure this is one of them."

Voices drifted down to them. "We should maintain silence, so no one realizes we're coming," she said, dreading what was ahead.

He sighed and nodded. Together, they inched down the narrow metal passage, trying to make as little noise as possible. It took a while to get anywhere, but gradually, the voices grew louder and louder until they stopped at a new opening. After shutting the light, they peeked through the slats of the grating.

As far as Cate could see with one eye, there were two people sitting in chairs in a small room cluttered with stuff. Both were guys who appeared to be either brutes or hard scroungers. Neither seemed like the sharing type. Grimacing, she glanced at Teddy, who didn't seem too happy.

"What now?" she mouthed, and he made a face.

"We wait," he mouthed back.

She couldn't tell if it was a statement or a question. Whatever he meant, she was too tired to quibble. Drained, she rested her head against her arms, closing her eye, legs stretched out behind her. In the stillness, she realized how near his body was to hers and how it was a strangely welcome uncomfortability. Did he notice too? Probably not. He didn't seem to pay attention to much not written down. She peered at him through a half-closed lid. He had put his head down too and seemed to be asleep. One of them should stay awake, but her eye closed. Exhausted, the warmth of the room laid a fog on her head. The voices drifted up to them. She tried to listen, but the words all blended in together, and she slept.

Chapter 6

In her dream, Cate stood outside enjoying a beautiful day. The wind tugged her hair, tossing strands everywhere about her. It felt good. The sun shone bright on her, warming her skin. Without warning, the heat began to hurt, burning, bubbling her skin. She stared as her hands swelled before her. The skin puckered and cracked, coming off in huge flakes and revealing dried muscle beneath. The fibers curled and turned black, peeling away from the stark white bone. Someone shook her. She wanted to scream, but her lungs burned too.

"Cate, Cate," hissed a voice near her ear.

Startled, she opened her eye and stared about her, bewildered. Teddy leaned in close, his face near hers.

"Hey, you're okay," he whispered.

"What are you talking about?" she hissed, embarrassed.

"You moaned in your sleep," he said, removing his hand from her back. "I might be wrong, but you didn't sound happy."

She shuddered, removing the last images of the dream from her mind. "Just an annoying dream. No need to be concerned."

He backed away. "I wasn't. I didn't want you to make any noise."

"Thanks for the warm fuzzies," she said, making a face at him. "Anyone still here?"

"The creepers left a moment ago. This is my old office above the warehouse floor as far as I can tell. I used to hang out here. We're in my old home as far as I can tell."

"This is good, yes?" she asked, yawning. Her body cramped from being in such an awkward space, and her hands had fallen asleep. "Wherever we are, let's get out of here."

He frowned but nodded. "Yeah. I think we're alone. Let's try to remove this cover quietly, just in case."

They pried the metal grate loose and dragged it into the vent. A light still shone in the room below which meant someone intended on coming back. Teddy inched forward and peered through the hole. He pulled his head back and moved forward, slipping his legs down. Lightly, he dropped to the desk below.

"Come on," he called, holding his arms out to her.

As she went through the hole, he caught her with ease, holding her for a moment longer than necessary with an odd glint to his eyes. Breathless, she backed away as a flush crawled up her neck.

"Okay, so now what? They obviously built a new way across the cavern." She hopped down from the desk. The room wasn't big with a window looking down into a vast space below. It was the warehouse. She never visited much before until the day they left the Undercity. However, she remembered lines of stuff, packed shelves, and cluttered floors. Now, the place held little more than piles of rubble.

"They've been digging," Teddy said, his face hard and eyes sad. "I think the place is empty, but we should be safe for the moment."

Teddy's movements around the place were second nature as he led the way down the stairs to the main area of his former home. Whatever they had left behind now lay in ruins. Pipes dangled from the ceiling, crude words sprayed across the walls, and anything left behind smashed or torn apart. He stood in the center of the room, his face reflecting hurt. It wouldn't take much to give comfort. All she needed to do was touch his shoulder. For a moment, she even raised a hand, but something inside made her stop. She brushed a hair from her face instead.

"So, what now?" she asked, leaning against a damaged stool.

He turned around, shaking himself. "Yeah, good question." He studied a fragment of a plate then chucked the piece aside. "Guess this stuff doesn't matter much anymore."

"Nope, never does," she said, clapping him on the back. "Right when you find a little segment to hold, someone comes along and rips it away."

"I'm sorry," he said and grasped her hands, rubbing her palms with his thumbs. "I'm sorry. I didn't understand before. Well, I kinda did, but in a 'yeah, I get it' kind of way. I shouldn't have pushed you to give up your space."

She lowered her gaze, slipping her hands away. "Eh, you get ideas in your head and focus." She slapped her hands together. "Then away you go," she laughed.

He stepped in and kissed her. His lips lingered on hers before he moved off, his face flushed. It happened so fast she had no defenses. For a moment, she did little more than stare at him. Her breath seemed caught in her chest. She licked her lips. They tingled.

"Well, um. See, you proved my point," she said with a shaky voice. She laughed, and he gave a rueful chuckle. "Your tunnels, we came to check if they found them?"

"Yeah," he said and twisted his hands behind his back as though he didn't trust them. "The entrance is that way," he told her, tilting his head.

"Lead," she said with a little shrug. He went ahead of her, and she took a full breath. Well, he did have pleasing assets.

Careful and quiet, they explored the rest of the warehouse, ever wary of being caught. No one was around. They found evidence the Upperlords searched the place, but the secret access to the tunnels was still intact.

Teddy studied the wall of rubble they sealed the entry with. "Well, I don't think they figured out this is where we went."

"Even if they did, this area is buried, all sealed from this end to the other, right? There is no way they could get through unless they spent all their time digging. I can't see them wanting to waste all their energy on that," she said, tossing a rock at the wall.

He clasped his hands to his hips. "Well, now we know."

"Yep."

"How about find a place to crash for a while," he said, running a hand through his hair.

She narrowed her gaze. "Yeah, crash. That's it, buddy," she told him with a wag of her finger.

"Come on," he said with a half grin. He tugged the sleeve of her shirt. "No worries."

No worries? She glowered at him. "Hey, you're the one doing the kissing."

His chuckle held a hint of embarrassment. "I would like to say I planned to kiss you," he admitted, "but it surprised me too."

"Is that a good thing or bad? Did you want to kiss me? Or was it a fluke of the moment?"

"Can I answer that when I'm certain which answer will make you happy?" he asked, backing away.

She caught sight of something moving behind him. "Chicken."

"At the moment, yes."

"No, chicken," she repeated, pointing to the bird huddled in a box.

He whirled around and laughed. "Chicken."

"Supper?"

Teddy's eyes sparkled. "You go that way, and I'll cover this end." He gestured to the left.

"That's my blank side," she said and went the other way.

"Right, sorry," he muttered.

"And then what?" she asked as she moved, careful not to disturb their prey.

He lunged for the chicken, which squealed and jumped, her feathers flying. Teddy landed with a thud. Cate scrambled to catch her foot, but she was frantic now. The creature half-climbed, half-hopped over a lump of rubble. She tripped over a wire and fell beside her prey, which pecked at her in retaliation. Teddy made a wild grab. The poor thing screeched and flapped hard, leaving him holding nothing, but two long feathers. Cate snagged a tarp crumpled up beside her. She inched toward their quarry, which lunged itself into a corner. Teddy, sweating and dirty, moved around the other side. He found an old sheet and held it out before him. The bird's eyes were wild, her beak open. For a moment, Cate felt sorry for her, but food was food, and she was too hungry to get soft.

"Haaaa," she yelled and dropped her tarp on their chicken who squawked and wrestled in protest. Finally, she grabbed the creature by the neck. Cate blew strands of hair out of her face.

Teddy stepped away; his face lost all colour and his brows knitted together. "Ah, I'm gonna find something to cook with."

She made a face at him. "You're not going to tell me you can't kill a chicken."

He gave a tight, helpless grin and scuttled away. She stared at the pathetic bird in her hands and tightened her grip. "Sorry, bird. It's eat or be eaten," she said and twisted. The creature made one more squeak, and fluttered about, her head bobbling on her body. In a moment, the chicken fell still, and she set to plucking the feathers. Mrs. Fish said the job was easier to do if she soaked the body in boiling water first, but they did not have that luxury.

Teddy wandered back a little while later with a large pot in his hands. He cleared away pieces of broken furniture and put the pot on the cement. After, he dumped a bunch of paper, cardboard, and other flammables in and held up a little box. "Found a pack of Ma's matches. There are only a couple left, but I should be able to get things going for us."

"Yay," she replied and spit out a feather, which floated everywhere, tickling her nose and getting in her hair.

A strange grin spread across his lips.

"What?"

"You're pretty in feathers," he laughed.

She tried to chuck some at him. "Don't tease or you can do this, and I'll tend the fire. Where do you think the chicken came from?"

"Good question," he said as he fed the fire. "Ma got a couple from Georges before. Perhaps this one escaped from one of the Underlings we brought across."

"Well, wherever the poor bird came from, I won't complain. I'm hungry," she said as she cleaned the body out and put the carcass over the fire.

Caden hid under her blanket. The day was entertaining, but she reached her limit. Deb teamed up with Henri, and they traded off reading, each even threw in different voices and tried acting out several scenes. The brute was kind as always, smiling and gentle. His eyes sparkled so much, and he seemed so happy; did he like her that much?

They were gone now, and the room was silent. She relaxed her body. The ache wasn't so bad anymore. She moved without wincing. Restless, she got up and eased into some pants and a shirt. Activity didn't seem too bad either. A walk would be good. She ate supper earlier, courtesy of Henri. Quietly, she slipped out of the room and meandered toward the stairs. Her thoughts drifting back to Teddy and Cate.

"If you wander away, Ma will spit stones."

She pivoted around, startled by the comment. Jolon leaned against a doorframe, waiting.

"So will Henri," he added as he meandered over. "So, where you off to?"

Frowning, she shook her head. "Nowhere special. Needed to move about."

"I was thinking of drifting down to the bookstore, myself," he said with his eyebrows raised. "Wanna drift with me?"

"Why do you want to go there?" she asked with suspicion. He was an odd little fellow with too many corners where he kept secrets. Still, she adored him as a brother. Jolon always brought an interesting twist to any situation.

"Just do."

"Ma cut you off from snacks?"

"Sort of," he admitted, his cheeks tinting purple. "Might be I want a book."

"Right. Fine. It's as good a place to go as any," she said as she patted him on the shoulder.

They snuck out of the tower and through the sunrise room. The hour was late, and few people lingered around. Nobody paid attention as they wandered to the stairs and disappeared.

"You sure you up to this?" Jolon asked, and she nodded.

"Good to go," she assured him, and it was true, almost. Her limbs worked with minimal pain, and her breathing came with ease. Life rarely got better. "Where do you think they are?" she asked before realizing Jolon didn't know the others had left. She bit her lip, trying to come up with a way to cover up the mistake.

"Don't know. Probably lost in the ventilation system, knowing Teddy. Either that or Cate has done him in and found a whole new home to live in."

She stared at him. "Who told you?"

"Yeah, that's the trick," he said as they descended the last stairwell. "You guys tend to think you keep secrets from me, but I always find out. I'm resourceful that way."

"Okay, I'll give you that, but Teddy, Cate, and I were the only ones in the room."

He paused as they came to the bookstore. "Simple. I followed them." His grin was wide and mischievous. She laughed with him, and they went into the building. "Not too far, mind you, but I understand how Teddy works. He gets something under his skin, and away he goes. And he always drags somebody with him. I'm just glad it wasn't me this time."

"So, do you know why they went?" she asked as she lit a few candles. The glow radiated around the room, casting shadows everywhere.

"Don't you?"

"Yeah, I just wondered how much you worked out."

He sat down at a desk, putting his feet up. "Well, I figured when Teddy heard about the noise at the tunnels, he would get all curious. So, I figured he would check things out. It's kinda silly to me. Uppercity has nothing I would want to go back to, but I'm not Teddy."

"Yeah," she said absently, her thoughts dwelling on her other brother.

"Maybe it's 'cause he got tall in the last couple of months, but he's not the same since we got here. I mean, he is, but he isn't, right?"

She gazed at her little brother. They all changed since they moved. The cozy family depending on each other was not quite so cozy anymore. Cate was right. Change was good, but sometimes one lost things during the process.

"Yeah," she said and gazed about the room. Books packed with so much information—so much change—filled every corner and shelf. "I guess things will keep changing, won't they? Hey, how about we do something for..."

"There you are," said a deep voice.

She turned around and faced Henri, who stood at the entrance with a lantern and a disapproving pout on his face.

"Hey, big guy." Jolon held up a cookie wrapped in plastic. "You want one?"

He didn't appear impressed.

"Henri. You followed us," she said more irritated than fearful of his disapproval.

"Yes," he said, shaking a finger at her. "And you..."

"Shouldn't be out of bed," she finished with a disparaging tone. "You are not my Ma, Henri, and I'm fine. I needed to move. So don't get all ruffled. Eat your cookie."

For a moment, his face shifted as he struggled with what to do. He snatched the package from Jolon before plopping down on a chair. "Still wrong," he muttered and bit into the food.

"You were saying..." Jolon said, amused.

Caden stared at him. "Ah, we should do something special for Cate. She's giving up her spot so Teddy can build his school......"

"I thought we were going to put the school in the tower?"

"I guess so," she said, restless to do something. Something pulled at her, something she couldn't define. "It would just be...."

"Something to do?"

She frowned at her brother. "Good."

"What good you want?" Henri asked, and she grinned at him. "Actually, it's perfect you're here." He lit up and blushed. "We will need your muscles," she added, pulling back her smile and putting up her hands.

He gave a half shrug. "It start."

Jolon chortled. "Okay, so what's the good you want to do?"

She gestured toward the back room. "If we clean the room up, we might make a pleasant place for Cate to live."

"Good plan," Henri said. He got to his feet and went off toward the storage room.

Caden stared at Jolon, her eyebrows raised with expectation. He groaned and got to his feet.

"Fine, fine. Good, good. I suppose it's better than sitting around."

They followed Henri into the room and stared at the mess.

Jolon screwed up his nose at the stench. "Ack, we're never getting the cats or the cat stench out of here," he said as a tabby wound itself around his legs.

Henri set a shelf on its feet. "We take junk out. Then scrub down. Cats go away on their own." He put his words into action and dove into the work "You do nothing," he went on. "He and me we take care."

"Well, that's not fair," she protested. "What am I supposed to do? Search for decorations?"

"Good idea. Easy. You be okay."

"How about she helps you, and I hunt for the decorations?" Jolon suggested.

The brute thrust a box at him. "You lift. Do you good. Make muscle."

"Right, like that's all I need."

Henri laughed as he worked and Jolon did as ordered. Caden considered ignoring the brute for a moment, frustrated at being left out. She supposed Henri was right; she wasn't too strong at the moment no matter what she wanted to believe. Still, decorating didn't rate high on her list of pleasures. She wandered out into the store while Henri piled boxes and bins of books in a free corner. She searched through them, taking out a few things Cate might like.

The cats screeched in protest, but the other two ignored the creatures. Jolon chased a few out of his way, and they scattered, disappearing into the vents and running into the store. Caden shooed a few out into the stairwell.

It took several hours, but they hauled a lot of the garbage and other stuff out. She was tired and depressed. The fatigue crept in as it always did when she was unwell, a deep ache, which had no relation to physical pain, an unsettled weariness which never went away. She slumped down on a low stool and surveyed the place. The walls were stone behind her and painted wallboard on the other three. The room was dank with stains everywhere and no windows. Perhaps the idea wasn't so good. Maybe there was no way to make the place pleasant. She turned up the flame on the lamp Henri brought.

"So, where does the door go?" she asked, noting the entrance behind a tall cardboard cut-out of two people entwined.

"Don't know," Henri said, coming over. He tossed the cut out aside.

"We shouldn't," Jolon interjected as Henri put his hand on the bar. "Might not be good."

She was about to agree when she detected scrapes on the floor. The marks were fresh as though someone went through the door recently, dragging something behind them. "Someone's been here," she said, pointing at the floor.

"Teddy?" Jolon asked.

"No, he would have told us," she decided with a quick shake of her head. "No, I'm guessing Cate. She's the only one who would go through doors without preparing first."

"So, it safe?" Henri asked.

She traded glances with Jolon and shrugged. "She was living the last time I saw her."

"Cheerful thought." Her brother waved at Henri. "Well, go on. Push."

He did as told while she picked up the light and went forward.

"Oooh, exciting, an alley," Jolon said, dryly.

"Alley?" Henri asked as they searched around.

"Yeah, that's what Teddy calls this kind of thing," he said with a sigh as though explanations bored him. "This would have been outside, but there was so much debris that it made a tunnel. Found places like this all over Undercity. They collapse after a time. Unstable."

Caden wandered about, trying to decide if anything inside was useful. A part of a car stuck out of the rubble on one side. That wasn't much use unless the tank still held some gas which she doubted. Finger marks covered the glass. Cate. Caden turned around and spied a door in the other building. It was shut, but drag marks showed on the ground like someone had pulled something through to the other side. Curious, she turned the knob.

"You're not worrying about anything these days, are you?" Jolon asked, joining her.

"Cate's been through here," she said and continued searching the hall. Most of the doors were closed. Light poured through one, and she approached the opening with care.

Henri pressed gentle fingers to her forearm. "Easy."

She rolled her eyes. "Yes, dear," she said without thinking how he would take the endearment. "That's a facetious 'dear,' buddy. Don't make it into anything else."

His face was stoic and solid aside from the twitching in the corners of his lips. "K."

Annoyed, she punched his arm, hurting her fingers more than anything else. Shaking her hand, she went into the apartment. The room was pretty with a soft couch and a collection of trinkets and books on shelves. A cat scooted by her feet and she jumped. Henri caught the lantern she almost dropped. He lifted the glass and blew out the light.

"No need. Bright room," he said and put the lamp on the counter.

Her brother stood in the kitchen, rummaging through the cupboards. He held up a couple of food cans. "Cate must be staying here. Emptied recently."

"Not surprising. Cate always finds the good hiding spots."

"But why pretend? Why get uptight about the alcove? This doesn't make any sense," Jolon asked, tossing the can back in the sink.

"Because it's hers."

"Kitty wants out," Henri said, and Caden turned back to him.

The cat pawed at the glass door. She went to the creature and petted the tiny orange head. The courtyard beyond was beautiful. She had never seen flowers like these before. The blossoms were the size of her hand and as colourful as Teddy's best picture books. "It's amazing," she breathed, awed.

Jolon came beside her. "We can't let kitty out."

"No," she said and gasped as another cat appeared on the other side of the glass. The black feline stared up at them and licked its paw. She gaped at the creature. It was outside, breathing, and alive.

Stunned, she stepped back, barely noticing the other two did the same. Jolon stared at the animal, his eyes like white globes. Henri fidgeted on the other side of her, flexing his hands and licking his lips.

"We can't go out, can we?" Jolon stared at her, his round face pale. "We can't. I mean it. We can't." He turned his gaze back to the glass door. "Well, perhaps... no.... No. Of course not. This is nonsense. No."

Caden frowned, annoyed with her little brother. She shook her head and grabbed the handle to the door, opening it with one strong pull. The other two shouted in alarm before they all went silent, waiting as the wind touched them.

One cat came in, and the other one went out. Caden breathed the fresh air. It didn't hurt or didn't do anything, except smell pure and feel good. She stepped forward; Henri seized her arm.

"No."

She smiled at him and took his fingers away. The square space was so beautiful. She stepped out, following the animal into the sunlight. Amazed, she turned and laughed. They stared at her as though they expected her to melt.

"Come on," she said, beckoning them.

They gawked as though she was ten cookies short of a dozen before Henri ventured out too. Jolon shook his head.

"Well, I guess this is as good a way to go as any," he muttered and joined them.

Henri handed Caden a pink flower with white stripes and a nutty scent. She couldn't help herself; she felt so good she hugged him. He blushed and giggled.

"We did it," she said, shaking out years of darkness as the warm sun's rays drenched her skin. "We are outside."

"And alive," Henri added, his face glowing.

"And not boiling into ashes," Jolon said with a scowl. He hunched over as though expecting to fry at any time.

"Don't think you can boil to ashes," Henri said, looking confused.

She started to laugh, a bubbly giggle, which welled up in her stomach and spilled out in uncontrolled joy. The laughter was catching, and soon all three of them collapsed, clutching their abs.

As the giggles subsided, they all lay on the grass staring up at the endless space above them. The wind teased her, caressing her, and bringing new fragrances to her nose. Caden sighed.

"This is more incredible than I ever imagined," she said, enjoying the heat on her skin.

"I never tried to imagine it," Jolon said.

"Not once?"

"No. Not once. Too terrifying. All the space—I couldn't go there. But this, this isn't so bad. If we were out in the vast green that seems to go on beyond sight, yeah, I would be hiding under something."

Henri put his hands behind his head. "Walls make safe."

Caden gazed again at the weaving mass of vegetation surrounding them. It was true. If the apartment had faced an open field, she doubted she would have gone out the door. This was safe. This was contained.

"Do you think Cate went out here? Do you think she knows?"

She held her hand out to the kitty who wandered around them. "I would say yes. Otherwise, how did the cat get out?"

"Unless it isn't Cate?"

Caden stared at her brother. "What do you mean?"

"We assumed Cate opened the other door and found this place, but what if it's someone else?"

A chill ran through her, making her shoulders twitch. Henri got up, his gaze intense as he scanned the area. "We get back inside," he said, and they agreed.

They scrambled back, shutting the glass door behind them. Caden sunk down on the greyish blue couch, her heart pounding.

"No, it was Cate. Had to be," she said, trying to convince herself. We haven't seen signs of anyone else."

"We leave in case," Henri suggested, checking the rest of the apartment as though he expected some kind of monster to jump out at him.

"Yeah," Jolon said and scampered out the door.

Caden followed, reluctant to leave the place behind. Henri came up behind her with the lantern in hand and closed the apartment door behind them.

"We go, we go," he rushed, the light swinging about.

They got back into the storage room, and the boys blocked the entrance. All three of them sat down. Caden felt like she was on fire; she was so wired.

"We can't leave this," she said, staring at the shelf they shoved in front of the door. "We were outside."

"Who was outside? Outside what?"

All three of them turned. Deb stood by with a biscuit in one hand and a book in the other. She held out the cookie to Jolon.

"This thing is hard. How can you eat these?"

"Outside the door," Caden said quickly, hoping to satisfy their little sister. "We went out into the back."

"So?"

Jolon grabbed her cookie. "I dunk them in hot tea. Come on, I'll make some for you." He turned her about and escorted her back to a table cluttered with children's books.

Caden slipped back down on her seat, a wave of weakness coursing through her. Henri put a hand on her shoulder, and she didn't bother pushing him away.

"You need rest," he said, square face all concerned. He helped her to her feet and supported her as they left. "I take you back."

She was spent now. All the excitement from being outside came crashing in on her. Was she all right? She dared to go out into the sunlight. Perhaps she wasn't. She studied Henri, who seemed okay, a little flushed, but his usual blocky self. Everything was fine. It was all fine. She was exhausted. Leaning on him, she let him take her home. The others followed with cookies and bags for tea.

They all went to her room. Jolon made everyone something to drink, and they gathered on the beds, dunking biscuits and sipping hot ginger. Everyone avoided discussing their adventure by keeping the conversation centred on books and the school. Deb seemed most interested in her cat, which curled up on her bed and swatted at a ragged length of string. After the boys had left, they got ready for bed. Her sister was so quiet it made her thoughtful. No, she decided as she settled for the night. All was good.

The next morning, Caden woke to an empty room. Sunlight filtered in around the curtains, making the room a dusty blue. She slept in.

Every day Deb got up early and went to their mother, so her bed was empty except for Mr. Poufy, who stretched and cried for food. She was a restless child who found it hard to stay in one spot. Caden didn't worry about her. Content, she contemplated getting out of bed. Her night's sleep had been good though her dreams were vivid and filled with flowers. Gingerly, she rotated her legs around and stood. Okay, not too bad. She was a little light in the head, but that wasn't unusual first thing in the day.

After snatching up a towel, she went into the bathroom and showered. The water was warm as usual. They still hadn't quite got things to where a person might enjoy a consistent hot soak. However, it was a wonderful change from sharing bath water in a tin tub once a week.

After she got out, she rubbed her skin dry and got dressed, throwing on a pair of dark trousers and a dress shirt which was too big for her. She tucked the excess material in and rolled up the sleeves. Someone knocked at the door. Probably Ma and Deb with her breakfast.

"Good morning, Love," her mother greeted as she entered and gave her a peck on the cheek. She placed the tray she carried down on the small table. "Here are some fried veggies and grilled potatoes."

"Thanks," she said and took a seat. Her stomach grumbled as the delicious fragrance entered her nose. "Where's Deb?"

Her mother checked around the room. "I thought she was here."

Caden paused in her eating. "No."

"Oh, she probably went to the sunroom with Mrs. Fish's little ones. They were going to plant some new seeds they found," her mother told her as she sat on the bed. "You seem better."

"I'm feeling better too," she said and hurried to finish her food. "I'm going to try spending a little time with the flowers too, today."

Ma nodded, smiling. "Good idea. The sun is good for you. I think Henri and Jolon are there too. I haven't seen Teddy around, though. Actually, I haven't seen him since yesterday morning."

"Ah, he spent yesterday in the bookstore," Caden said. "I suspect he fell asleep under a horde of books."

Her mother rose to her feet. "I'm must visit this wondrous bookstore soon. When you see your brother next, tell him, would you?"

"No problem," she said. "I'll commission Henri and Jolon to find him for you."

After her mother left with the empty tray, Caden put on some socks and her shoes and left to find the others. She hoped Deb was with them, but she had a growing dread her little sister wandered where she shouldn't.

Chapter 7

Cate woke with a start, sitting up quickly. It took a moment to recognize where she was. After tossing aside the tarp she covered herself with, she crawled over to Teddy and shook him. He moaned and muttered as he woke. She put a hand over his mouth and a finger over her own lips as he opened his eyes.

"Someone's here," she whispered, leaning in close.

Carefully, she peered around the pile of junk they hid behind. The two men were back. Teddy came up beside her and they both spied on them.

"One more day sifting through this junk," the taller one complained, shoving a broken table aside. He was a broad shouldered brute built like a tapered block with pants too short and feet to big. "Don't seem to me this dump has much left worth scrounging out."

The shorter one was skinny with limbs like sticks. His face was scarred and twisted as though he received one too many beatings. "Eh, don't get why we got to spend our days slummin' around here as though anyone's gonna come back. I figure them who were here are dead now. Nowhere else for them to go. I figure they tried to escape through some tunnels and the whole thing collapsed on them. Otherwise, we would find a sign a them."

The wedge pulled out a flask and leaned against the partial remains of a shelf. "Could be worse. This is a cush job. All we gotta do is find a little extra company of the softer, sweeter variety and we got the life."

"Softer variety? Sweeter?" Sticks mocked. "Ain't too many a them left now. At least, none for the likes of us." He snatched the flask from Wedge and took a long drink. "Gah, this stuff is pure poison," he spat, choking.

"Ya don't like it, don't drink," Wedge told him, snatching the flask back. "I spend months makin' this stuff, scrounging for bits to put in. It's the only thing keeping me sane in this hell." He took a long swig and snapped the lid back on, stuffing the bottle in his shirt.

"Keeping you sane? Right. More like helping you eat your own brain."

They wandered back to the little office Teddy told her was his old hideout. Cate slid down and mushed her face with her hands. "Oh, this isn't good," she muttered. "Why did we sleep here? We should have at least gone back in the vent. Now we're stuck."

Teddy slumped beside her. "Yeah, well. I think we were both a little too weary and full of chicken to think right."

She chuckled. The chicken. They had fun chasing the poor bird about. She had no problem wringing the creature's neck, though Teddy left. He seemed squeamish about killing for a boy from Undercity. However, he was resourceful and built a crude fire pit. He even made a spit over the flames. Plucking the bird had been the worst. They both came out enveloped in feathers.

"Do you think they'll stay all day?"

He shrugged. "If they do, we're stuck here all day. There isn't anywhere else we can go anymore."

Quiet and careful, she scooted over to the fire, making certain it was out. A pressure in her bladder reminded her she needed to relieve herself, but where? She preferred not getting caught with her pants down so she searched for some place out of view of anyone.

She pointed to a corner sheltered by a dilapidated cabinet. Teddy nodded as he got the picture. At least, she hoped he understood. As quickly as she could without making noise, she crawled in behind the furniture and released her water. It was a challenge to crouch amid the trash with her pants around her ankles and pee slow enough not to make a sound. Fervently, she hoped she wouldn't get her clothes wet. When she finished, she crept back to their spot and Teddy took his turn. He came back moments later, and they both crouched down, watching for the other two.

"This won't work," she muttered. "We're both hungry, tired, and thirsty. We can't sit the day out here, waiting."

He nodded, looking anxious. "Yeah. My family will worry if we don't show up soon too, and I don't think Caden will be able to stall them until we get back."

"So, what do we do?" She had no desire to get near those creepers. They were the kind that wouldn't hesitate to use her if they caught her. Searching around, she grasped a heavy pipe— she wasn't about to let that happen.

Teddy expression turned disapproving.

"Yeah?" she hissed, handing him a pipe. "You wait, pretty boy. You think those two are gonna stop with me?"

His frown deepened, but he grabbed the weapon. "No, and even if they would, they aren't touching you."

She understood he meant his vow sincerely, but it was so heroic, she couldn't help chuckling. She hid it under a clearing of the throat.

"So, now what? Draw 'em out and crack 'em on the head?" she asked, testing the weight of her pipe.

"I hoped to avoid cracking anyone," he said, peering out over the warehouse again. "Our best bet might be to slip out over the new bridge and find another way back."

This didn't sound like a good alternative. To go back to Undercity would only lead to more trouble. "You are kidding, right?" Do you realize how long that would take? Besides, we won't blend in. Not now. They will recognize your pretty face."

"Why would they know me? It's not like they would have a picture and a poster. Those kinds of skills went out with the rest of the world. Besides, I grew a foot since we left, and don't call me pretty."

She shook her head. "All right, fine. So they won't remember you, but we already know there isn't a way out that way unless you are hiding another secret passage. And don't blame me that you're pretty."

"I kinda think you're both pretty," said a voice which made them freeze. They turned. Wedge stepped out from behind a pile of garbage. "At least, pretty enough to satisfy." A crooked smirk spread across his face as he laughed. Sticks joined him, snickering.

Cate and Teddy huddled together, holding their respective pipes up.

"Aw, come on, little chickies, no need to be so standoffish. Me and him, we're friendly types." They both grinned, their rotting teeth disgusting.

"Yeah, well, we're not," Cate snarled and feigned a swing at Stick's head. As he raised his arms, she caught him in the ribs. He fell into Wedge with a grunt. Teddy jumped in and jabbed Wedge in the stomach as the creeper faltered on some rubble. Cate swung again, hitting Sticks hard on the back.

"Come on," Teddy shouted as he smacked Wedge's head. They scrambled over the junk and headed toward the stairs. If they got back into the vents, they might get away.

Caden found Henri and Jolon hanging out in the sunroom. Her brother sat on a stone planter, munching on something while Henri puttered with a few plants.

"Is Deb with you?" she asked, rushing up to them.

"Is she supposed to be?" Jolon asked as Henri shook his head.

"She wasn't around this morning when I woke up. Ma figured she was down here." She wrung her hands and chewed on her lips.

"You afraid," Henri said, and she nodded.

"I don't think our explanation yesterday satisfied her. I think she heard us talking about outside."

"Yeah, but even if she did, there's no way she could move the bookshelf we stuck in front of the door," Jolon said, getting to his feet.

Caden leaned in close. "Yeah, but...but there are other ways out, right? If she got the thought in her head to go outside..."

"She would find way," Henri finished.

"Yeah," Caden said, nodding. A lump of lead settled in her stomach at the thought.

"So, where do we search?" Jolon asked, his eyebrows woven together in fear.

She shrugged. "Good question."

Henri touched her arm with a tentative gesture. "Where door easy to find?"

Jolon snapped his fingers. "The bookstore."

"We blocked that one; the rest of the place is under dirt."

He shook his head. "No. There's a door in the kitchen part. I found it when checking for food. She knows it is there, 'cause she came back with me. It's not blocked or anything."

"Could she open it?" she asked.

"Don't know," he said, twitching. "But we should check."

"She reading in kid's section surrounded by stuffs and munching stale cookies," Henri offered with a hopeful nod.

"She better be. We gotta find her." Caden's legs ached and joints throbbed with pins of pain, but she didn't care. She rushed off with the others anyway.

The building was silent when they entered. If she came there, they found no sign.

"Deb? Deb!" Caden called, and the others joined in. "Where's this door?" she asked Jolon, and he pointed toward the back of the kitchen area.

"In through here." He led the way through a swinging door into the back. The room contained several shelves and a couple of metal counters. A slit of light drifted in through a small window in a door in the back wall. They had no way of telling if Deb went through it.

"So, what now?" Jolon asked, breaking the silence.

Caden tapped a hand against her leg. "We open it. Something might be on the other side."

"I go first," Henri said, his brave face on. He twisted the handle and pulled. The sunlight poured in, bright and warm as he dragged the door wide open. Grass waved high right up to the moss covered cement walkway.

"Footsteps," Caden breathed, noting the line of sunken prints, which cut a trail through the grass. They glanced at each other.

"Okay, I guess we follow," Jolon said.

"Yeah," Caden said, her heart in her throat. She didn't know what made her take Henri's hand, but she felt more secure as his fingers curled around hers. They walked out together, the sunlight making all three of them squint. The wind whirled around them, filling the air with the scent of grass.

Terror and elation mixed together in Caden. Her breath quickened as her heart thumped wildly. Only concern for Deb kept her from bolting back into the shelter she understood.

"How far do you think she got?" Jolon asked, looking uneasy and somewhat green.

Unlike the courtyard, this was an open field heading away from the bookshop and stretching out to the horizon. Buildings jutted from the ground in places like decaying skeletons. Many missed walls and windows. A few still stood though the vegetation seemed to be determined to take them over. Poles stuck into the air, covered in vines. Smudges of billowing clouds floated high in the blue, some pure white, others slate grey. Lumps of what had to be vehicles buried in dirt and grass cluttered the land. All this made searching for signs of Deb difficult. It also made their trek more hazardous as the unstable ground made their feet sink.

"Deb!" Caden continued to call out. "This is ridiculous. Where can she be?"

"Well, we follow trail," Henri said, his lips in a grim line. "It all we got."

"Deb! Silly child, where are you!"

Jolon scrubbed at his scalp. "Perhaps you shouldn't shout so loud," he said, his face a picture of terror. "We have no idea what's out there."

"Doesn't matter," she said, her fears growing. "Deb is out there, our 'little' sister and we don't know what's out there with her."

"That's just it. We don't know what's out there with her and we don't want anything that might be out there to be drawn to either us or her by the shouting."

She threw dark eye-daggers at him, hating it when he made sense. "Yeah, fine. I guess that way we can hear her too. Here, brute-guy, help me up." She held out a hand and steadied herself with Henri's help as she climbed up a mound. It seemed stable enough and the height offered a better view. Far off behind them stood home and the security of the bookstore. Despite the desire to run back the way, she searched for any sign of movement. "There," she said, pointing to where the greenery seemed thicker. She scrambled down, and they continued on, following the trail and moving toward a thick forest of bush and trees.

"Little girl fast," Henri puffed as they scrambled to catch up to her.

"She's small, she can weave through this stuff easy." Caden struggled with the vegetation. The hot and muggy air was heavy and difficult to breathe. A momentary fear crept in, making her doubt the quality of the air. Maybe it was poison, eating their lungs? A rumbled boom came from above them. The hairs on the back of her neck prickled.

"Rain, yes?" Jolon said, eyes round and face ashen. "That's what Teddy described in his books... a rumbling." He smacked the side of his head as though trying to dislodge a memory. "Th... thunder. That's it. That's all it is."

"Yes," Caden agreed though the realization did not give comfort. "Right. We've heard it before inside the tower."

"Not so scary," Henri added, and they all gave an uncomfortable chuckle.

"If it is rain, we better get Deb then get back as soon as we can," Caden decided, wishing the golden child hadn't wandered so far so fast. "She must have snuck out early this morning to get all the way out here."

They came to a line of low trees and lost her trail.

"Damn it, Deb, where are you?" Caden shouted, hands to her mouth. Her eyes stung, and she took a deep breath as desperation threatened to make her cry. Disgusted with the panic threatening to engulf her, she clenched her jaw and pushed the emotions aside. Tears had no point and wouldn't help anything.

"We should have brought some supplies," Jolon said, holding his side as he caught his breath.

"Oh, your stomach will survive," Caden growled more harshly than she meant.

"It's not my stomach I'm worried about," he said, his tone angry and hurt. "If you haven't noticed, the sky is getting darker, and the wind is getting stronger. I don't know much about the outside, but I know trouble coming when I sense it. That is trouble." He pointed up at the gathering clouds low in the sky. The sickly greenish grey mass hid much of the sunlight.

"We need to find Deb first, then find shelter. 'Cause I don't think anything coming out of that will be fun." He shoved his hands in his pockets, his face close to tears. "And we need water and, yes, I'm hungry. Okay? I'm hungry and it's not a crime. I'm scared too 'cause I lost track of where we are in relation to home."

A soft string of curses escaped her as she gazed around. She had been so intent on finding her sister, she lost sight of where they were. Every which way she turned she faced a wall of thick green vegetation. She put an arm around Jolon.

"The bookstore was behind us before—or to the left. No, behind us and to the right. We'll figure this out. Don't worry. Don't be scared."

He wiped his face with his sleeve. "Too late."

She chuckled, patting his head.

Henri hugged them both from behind. "I keep you safe," he vowed in his serious voice. "We fix this."

They stayed that way for a moment longer before Caden pushed away from them. "As cozy as this is, we aren't getting anywhere. I figure we have three, no four choices. One, we keep going and hope to find Deb before the storm hits. Two, we stay here and hunker down until the storm is over. Three. we try to get home and hope to get back before the storm flattens us. Or, four, we try to find some kind of shelter and hope Deb is doing the same thing."

"Those are terrible choices," Jolon said as he calmed down.

The wind came up, stronger, pushing at them and bending the trees hard. Above them, the clouds started to swirl in a writhing knot.

"I say shelter," Henri said, even he seemed kind of scared.

"Yeah," Jolon agreed, hugging himself.

Caden nodded, hating the idea which meant leaving Deb on her own, but they had no clear idea where she was. "So, Deb went off that way as far as we can tell." She ran a finger along a vague trail leading through the thicket. "Here's what I figure. We follow and keep a lookout for a good place to hide. If luck manages to help us, we'll find both Deb and shelter."

They agreed and took off at a good pace. Drops of icy rain started to fall as did the temperature of the air. While the storm picked up, they struggled through the brush, the wind loud in their ears. Caden's body ached, every muscle protesting the exertion. For a moment, she feared they chose the wrong path, but the foliage gave way to a wider opening which was long and straight with patches of pavement. Far down the way, Caden caught a momentary glimpse of movement. She quickened her pace despite the protests of her body.

"Deb!" she called and Henri rushed on ahead. A stab of pain coursed through her back. She gasped and slowed to a walk despite herself. Spots whirled in front of her eyes and her head pounded.

"Don't worry, don't worry," Jolon said, slipping an arm around her. "I think Henri has Deb." He helped her over to the side, back among the trees.

They crawled to the top of a grassy mound. Caden held her head in her hands, tears streaming down her face, mixing with the rain. She shivered and Jolon huddled close.

"I got her," Henri huffed as he came back with a frightened Deb huddled in his arms.

Caden held her arms open and took her little sister. "You silly, silly girl," she scolded softly, and they both cried. Jolon snuggled in close, his eyes red.

"Stay here," Henri said, snuffling. "I go get shelter."

She wasn't sure if they consented or not. All she knew was she had her little sister back. The rain soaked them through and the wind made them huddle closer as the trees thrashed about. Dizzy as she was, she realized they couldn't stay where they were.

"Damn," she said, untangling herself from her siblings. "Where did he go? We shouldn't separate. The bloody hero. Where the…"

"I here, I here!" he said, stumbling through the bushes behind them. "Come." He took Deb from her and helped Caden get down.

They stayed tight with him as he guided them through the vegetation to a door almost hidden by branches.

"Get in!" he shouted over the roaring wind.

Stumbling, Caden hurried inside with Deb in front of her. Jolon followed with Henri coming behind. He hauled the door closed. The wood groaned under the force of his pull, but held. Exhausted, they all fell to the floor, lying in the grey twilight as the storm shrieked outside. Deb clung to Caden.

"I'm sorry," she whispered, trembling. "I only wanted to experience what outside was like."

"Shh, I understand." Caden stroked her wet hair. "It's okay."

Chapter 8

Teddy and Cate scrambled up the stairs and over the connecting landing. The two others picked themselves up and came after them, screaming obscenities. Cate grabbed Teddy as he paused to study something.

"Come on, dopy. This is not the time to find out how things work."

"I think we can break this," he said, indicating the landing. "Henri built it, but he only used a few nails." He swung his pipe at a weak spot. Wood splintered.

"Fine, you hit, I'll throw," she told him and snatched a rock from a pile by the door. They weren't big, but she figured they would slow the other two down. She threw the rock hard and caught Wedge on the arm.

"You damn hag!" he shouted, and she threw another.

Teddy swung again and again until the ledge wobbled. Cate threw everything she got her hands on at them.

"Hurry," she shouted. They were almost up the stairs. She gave up on throwing things and beat at the boards with him.

"Now, wait," said Sticks as he got to the other side. "We won't hurt you."

"Why do people say that? It's the most obvious lie in the world," Cate said, standing by Teddy, her pipe raised.

"Because the people who say it are the most ignorant people in the world," he grunted and gave the support one more immense whack. The landing creaked and snapped, half of it letting go.

"You bloody trash," Wedge growled, lunging forward.

It wasn't a good idea. The rest snapped and swung away, throwing him to the side. He clung to the edge, squealing. "Help! Help! Help!"

"I'll get you," Sticks said, trying to grab his friend as he swung back and forth.

"Come on," Cate said, pulling Teddy by the arm. "Let's go while we can."

They scrambled back into the office. She tossed the pipe aside and jumped on the desk while he got up beside her. He grabbed her around the waist and hoisted her toward the ceiling. She took hold of the edge, the metal biting into her hands. With a little work, she squirmed into the vent. After, she turned around and reached down for Teddy.

"Shit," he swore, looking toward the door. "They're gonna get across. All we did was slow them down."

"Well, come on," she snapped, gesturing to him.

He jumped for her hands, and she caught him, the strain sending spasms of pain through her shoulders. Grunting and swearing, she pulled hard, and he got a hold of the side. Fingers cramping, she seized the back of his shirt and hauled, struggling with his weight. Finally, he crawled over her. The tin creaked under their weight.

"I don't think this thing is made for this much abuse," Teddy gasped, working his way into the tunnel.

A loud crash from down below caught her attention. The creepers made it across and were trying to get up to them. She shoved the vent cover down, sharp corner first. The metal struck Wedge right across the face, gashing him.

"You scum rat!" he swore, holding a hand up to his face. "You will regret that."

Teddy pulled at her feet. "Come on."

She squirmed around and followed, crawling fast. They didn't have a flashlight anymore, and both packs were back in the warehouse, which wasn't good. Still, they had little choice.

Wedge and Sticks were still trying to get into the ductwork. Every move they made reverberated through the walls. A sickly groan accompanied a shudder and a crash. A quick glance back revealed that half the tunnel was gone and a gloomy patch of light filtered in. What happened to the other two, she didn't care. She kept on, keeping a hand near Teddy's foot.

For quite a while, they kept going despite not knowing where they were. There was no way to tell. They were either climbing around the floors of Uppercity, or somewhere in the malls, or somewhere completely different. Fatigue made her body want to stop while her throat ached and one eye blurred.

She paused, coughing as she hauled on Teddy's foot. "Stop," she croaked. "I gotta rest."

The tin tunnel clunked and banged as he crawled back to her, sneezing several times. His fingers brushed against hers, and she grasped them.

"Well, this is so much fun."

"Oh, yeah," he replied and coughed. "One adventure worth avoiding. This was such a bad idea. Both stashes are gone, we're lost, and, ahhh, I think I made things worse."

"What do you mean?" she asked, wishing she could see him.

"I think Belinda had given up on us. Now, they will know we're still around."

"But how? Or why? They might think we're stragglers from Undercity still looking for a way up."

She felt him shake his head. "We didn't leave that many stragglers behind. At least, none who understood scrounging like my family, and we had a reputation. Georges' sister knows how we worked. She'll figure it out. All it will take is a search of our packs."

"Perhaps, but they can't get through."

"No, but they can try to follow us. Now they know there's another way out."

"The vent behind us collapsed."

"They'll dig it out."

Both sat still for a moment—the only sound their own harsh breathing.

"What do we do?" she asked though she suspected she knew the answer.

"We lead them astray."

"Right," she said and shook his hand.

"Come on. I'm tired of this place. Let's head for the nearest shaft of light." He let go of her and kept going.

Shattered, she followed, thoughts flitting everywhere. Her stomach grumbled with empty cramps, and her muscles added several complaints. Still, they crept on.

"Anything?" she asked, hoping he saw something she couldn't.

"Not yet."

It was tough to say what turns they took to end up lost. The pipes were a maze, and they had no way of knowing which direction they faced. No sounds came from behind them, so there was a good chance Sticks and Wedge gave up for the moment.

"Hey," she gasped as she ran into Teddy's foot. "A little warning on the stopping."

"Sorry, but I think there's a light up ahead."

"Well, don't stop and ponder it," she said, flicking his boot. "Get moving."

They went forward again, and Cate got a good view of Teddy's backside, which was an enjoyable sight. Amused, she laughed at herself; she must be exhausted to find him attractive at that moment.

"Whoa." Unfortunately, he stopped as he spoke and she ran into him again.

"Hey, warning means letting someone know before you do something, smart boy," she growled, rubbing her nose.

"There's a way out," he said and inched his way forward. He swung around, put his legs through a hole, and disappeared. Seconds later a tremendous bang echoed through the tin tunnel.

"You alive?" she called out, crawling forward. Worried, she pulled her hair away from her eye and searched for him. Down below, he sat on the floor rubbing his ankle.

"Yeah," he grunted. "Think I twisted my ankle."

She swung down and dropped softly. "Perfect," she said and knelt beside him.

"Perfect as in 'that sucks' or as in 'a brilliant landing and that's how you should have done it'?" he asked, scowling with pain.

"A bit of both," she said with a shrug and a laugh.

"Thanks," he said and tried to stand.

"Whoops, not a good idea," she grunted as he fell against her. "Let's sit back down for the moment." She edged him over to a chair with wheels. The fickle seat tried to roll away, but she hooked the bottom with a foot as he grabbed hold of the back and crawled on. Once he stabilized, she searched around. Windows ran along the long end, and lines of little grey walls divided the room into strange boxes. Inside the boxes were desks and chairs, and a whole lot of other stuff she had never seen before.

"Ugly place," she said, putting Teddy's foot on the desk in front of them. "Stay here, I'll check for some supplies to help us."

"Be careful," he said, grimacing. "I'll keep an eye on the hole."

"Ooh, fun. Don't get too excited, old guy," she said as she walked away.

Everything was grey: the walls, floor, and all the furniture. The space oozed depressing. Many of the rooms had windows on the inside walls. It seemed odd to need to see in a room from the outside. Many stores in the mall had such display rooms, but they were showing off merchandise. What were they showing off here, paperwork or productivity? Curious, she went into one room and around the long oval desk sitting in the centre. Rain soaked the outer windows. She paused and put a hand against a glass pane, which chilled her fingers. The picture outside was a terrifying show of greenish grey clouds, violent winds, and lightning. Thankful to be inside, she turned away.

Ugly green cupboards lined the end wall. Chances were slim they held anything useful, but she checked in case of unexpected treasures. Most were locked, which seemed odd, as she couldn't think of a thing anyone would want to steal from a place like this. The others held a few cups and some rusted tins. She stepped back and her boot sunk into something squishy. Her breath caught—ratdog shit, a giant, fresh pile of ratdog shit. Damn.

Disgusted, she scraped the heel of her boot on a chair—very fresh ratdog crap. Worried, she twisted around, searching for the creature. Nothing, but now she recognized the gouges in the floor and walls, the piles of wiry black fur gathered in the corners, and the chew marks in the furniture. As she backed up, her heart beat faster.

"Teddy," she hollered as she ran into the other room. "Teddy, we gotta go." A sharp scuttling sound and a low growl came from behind her. Abruptly, sick yellow eyes appeared in the shadows, and the creatures moved forward, jaws dripping saliva. Desperate to get away, she wove through the cubbyhole offices, cursing and keeping an eye out for some kind of weapon as she went—paper, dust, and little plastic shelves—nothing to help them.

"Cate?" Teddy called, and he popped up, leaning on the chair.

"Ratdogs," she huffed and shoved him back on the chair. She whipped him around and pushed him through the maze of grey dividers.

"Whoa, what?" he yelped, his limbs flying. "Ah, hey careful of the foot!"

"Shut up and hold on."

Behind them, the ratdogs howled, a whining, desperate sound. Teddy grabbed the edge of the chair and pulled in his legs. "Where are we going?"

"Where, where, where? Good question," she shouted as she darted through the cubicles. Behind them, the clacking of the ratdog claws against the tiled floor spurred her on. "They're gaining on us," she said as the snarling and barking came closer.

"The door, the door," Teddy shouted, "head for the door!"

"What bloody door?" she shouted back, wishing her field of vision wasn't so limited.

"There, over there by that cabinet."

A ratdog charged as she pushed the chair around a corner. Teddy kicked at the creature, which squealed and flew to the side. Cate threw another kick as the demented animal tried to get up. It flew several feet and hit a wall.

She didn't care if the creature was dead. The rest of the pack of ratdogs following was almost upon them, and they had no weapons, no protection, only an exit leading to the unknown. Taking a deep breath, she charged ahead. With his good foot, Teddy hit the bar on the door, and they careened through the exit chair and all. For a second, they hung in the air before plunging downward and landing in a heap.

Cate gasped, forcing air into her lungs as icy rain poured over her. She got on her hands and knees, coughing. More than a dozen feet above, the door banged against a brick wall while ratdogs snarled and yipped, backing away from the downpour. Beside her, Teddy lay, groaning and clutching his leg. The chair was in pieces having broken upon impact with the grassy ground.

"Teddy. Teddy? You okay?" she managed as her lungs started working again.

"Uh, ahh, definitely not," he gasped.

She shook off her aches and crawled over to him. His wet face was ghostly with pain. "Perfect," she muttered.

The ratdogs at the door howled. Several of the feral beasts paced across the threshold, contemplating jumping down to get them. While swearing under her breath, she grabbed Teddy's arm.

"Hate to do this, but we gotta move before those things get brave. Come on. Lean on me."

"Ahhgnh," he moaned as she helped him to his good foot.

He leaned heavily on her and they hobbled away. Where they would go, she didn't know, but the only option she could see for them was to keep on moving.

"Gotta get inside," Teddy moaned. "The rain."

"Yeah, like I didn't realize. Don't worry, old guy, we start to melt, and your leg won't hurt anymore."

Rain continued to drench everything, making the ground uneven and slippery. The drenching downpour was so heavy strands of wet hair covered her eye. Functioning with only one eye already limited her sight. She didn't need this. Frustrated, she slicked her hair back and wiped at her face with her soaked sleeve. Something in the shape of a building stood a ways away. At least, the structure seemed rectangular as far as she could tell through the vegetation.

"There," she shouted, pointing as the wind almost knocked them over. They stumbled through long soaking grass, which wrapped around their legs and fastened to their pants. Huffing, Cate stopped and propped Teddy against a tree. His eyes closed tight and his face so pale his lips appeared fake on his face. "I think I've found a shelter hidden in the bushes. Stay here, I'll search for a way in."

He managed a nod, pressing his forehead against a branch while his fingers pressed white into the wood. Worried, she stepped away. The pain had to be bad for him to be so silent. The best way to help was to get out of the storm, so she tore at the vines and branches in front of her. After a fair bit of effort, she reached the outside of what looked like a weird sort of home.

The sides were some kind of metal, and the whole structure seemed to be set upon wheels. There were several windows; however, and she cleared away enough glass in front of a broken one to try getting inside. The shelter was dark, and she could barely discern the bench and table in front of her. With a tight hold on the edge for leverage, she hoisted herself inside with minimal damage to her skin. Fatigue made her shake as she checked for another way inside; Teddy would never get in through the window. A slit of light came through a crack in the ceiling and her vision adjusted enough to reveal a door in the opposite wall.

She ran her hands down the side until she found the handle and unlocked the door. It opened an inch, and she pushed harder. Each time she thrust her body against the stubborn metal, she gained a few more inches until the branches blocking her way broke, and she stumbled into the storm. Coughing and aching, she picked her way back to Teddy.

"Come on," she said, yelling to be heard over the din of the storm. "I got in." She looped his arm over her shoulders, and together they made their way back to the door. By the time they got inside, her strength almost gave out. Teddy crawled on a seat, and she pulled the door shut before falling into another, both of them panting.

Cate shuddered, soaked to the skin. After a moment, she got up and searched through the cupboards and closets. The floor plan was a strange setup with a bed in the back and even a bathroom and a kitchen area. Leaks in the roof left moulding tracks down the rotting walls. The space was small but probably made a pleasant home back before the world fell apart.

"Anything useful?" asked Teddy, his voice strained with pain. "Candles? Food?"

"Relax, hero, don't be so sensible."

A gust of wind rocked the shelter. A home on wheels no longer seemed like a clever idea. She snagged a bulky square cushion and stuffed it in the broken window, dulling the sound of the storm and blocking out some of the cold.

Teddy whimpered as he tried to get more comfortable. She knelt in front of him to check his foot. He went to pull away, but she gave him a stern glare. The state of his injury was not good. The ankle had swelled so much the shoe no longer fit. She untied the laces and slipped it off.

"Mmmmmhh," he whimpered, his jaw clenched and face perspiring.

"Sorry, shoe's gotta come off, though. Need some cold on this too. It's swollen and nasty looking." She pulled over a few more cushions and piled them up before propping his foot with care. "I'll be right back."

"Huh? Where are you... ahh," he yelped as he twisted his foot.

"Stay still and relax. I'll be back." She took a plastic bowl from a cupboard. "I'm going to put this out to collect rainwater, which should be cold enough to help."

The rain poured down so hard she dreaded going far, so she stuck the bowl under a stream running off a heavy bough. In seconds, it was nearly full. Drenched, she brought the water back in, leaving puddles in her steps.

"Oh, yuck. I always wondered what it would be like to be out in a storm, but this is a bit much." She put the bowl on the floor and placed his foot in the chilly water.

"Ah, yeah, that's unpleasant."

"It'll help. We'll have to get back to your Ma so she can bind it up properly. I'm not so clever at the nursing thing," she said as she sat back on her heels. "You should try and get some sleep."

"Right." He grimaced and rested back. Despite his wet condition and damaged ankle, his eyes closed in moments.

Cate studied him for a little while. He wasn't a bad sort. At least, she was getting used to him. The trip back to the tower was going to be trouble. In their hurry and fear, they left the stashes behind which meant surviving on what they could scrounge. She shivered and shuddered, her fingers icy. Warming up had to be her first concern; otherwise, neither of them would get back anywhere.

Caden held a sleeping Deb on her lap, the little girl's fingers wound tight into Caden's wet shirt. They cuddled in a large stuffed chair, and Henri found them a decent blanket. The wind picked up outside and snuck in through cracks in the walls and broken windows.

Henri crouched in the room trying to build a fire in a metal can he scrounged up. Jolon discovered a few candles and some matches, which he set up on a filthy table, the tiny lights dancing with the draft.

"Well, isn't this cozy," he said as he wrapped himself in another blanket and plopped on a damaged couch. A loud squeaking and scurrying accompanied the flurry of mice, which ran out from under the furniture. "Perfect," he muttered, pulling his feet in tight to his body.

"Yes," Henri exclaimed as the fire caught and flickered into warm flames. He fed a couple of pieces of broken furniture into it and sat back with a satisfied grin. "Now we warm."

He smiled at her, a sweet grin, kind and gentle. She liked him, yes, but not in the way he wanted. It was troubling to think of anyone in romantic terms not only because her health was unreliable, but also because she had difficulty seeing much of a future. Constant pain hindered her ability to reach out and get close to anyone or to think of any day beyond the one she was in.

"You find any food in your scrounging?" she asked Jolon.

Her brother shrugged. "Just a few remnants, bloated cans and such. Nothing good. Didn't bring anything either, sorry."

Thunder made them all jump as the wind burst through a splintered window and sent a shower of rain everywhere. Henri leaped up and grasped a busted cupboard door. He shoved the wood into the window frame and braced it with a tall lamp.

"Nasty, nasty," he said, wiping his face on his sleeve. He coughed and sat down beside Jolon. "We stuck here. Not good."

"The storm will end," Caden replied, holding Deb tight. "They always do. The fire's warming the place up, and we're dry here. All we have to do is wait."

The brute stretched and rubbed his face. "We sleep, morning good."

Jolon yawned. "Yeah, sleep. Good idea." He put his head against the arm of the couch and closed his eyes. In moments, he was snoring.

Deb squirmed on her lap, trying to get comfortable in her sleep. Caden winced as her little sister's elbow dug into her side.

"I put her on couch," Henri said and stood. Before Caden could object, he scooped Deb up and made her comfortable beside Jolon. The little girl mumbled something but stayed asleep. She sighed and stretched out.

Caden pushed her legs out in front of her, rubbing them. They tingled, and her calf muscles cramped.

"You okay?"

She nodded. "Yeah. Just tired. It's been a demanding day."

He chuckled. "I could rub," he offered as she worked the knots out of her leg.

"No thanks," she said, glancing at him.

A momentary flicker of hurt crossed his face. He sat down on the floor and put more fuel in the fire. "You don't trust me."

"I don't trust anyone, at least not much. That's the problem, Henri."

"You trust family."

She shrugged. "Yeah, I guess, but it has taken a long time, and I still don't trust them not to die or disappear, or anything like that."

"Me either." His voice was soft, and he stared into the flames. His broad, ruddy face was so expressive; he hid nothing.

"It's a terrible place to try and develop a relationship from," she said as she slid down beside him, warming her hands. "Some people can, I know, like Ma and Pa. They seem to have this endless well of stamina when it comes to loss. They recover, keep going, and seem to love all the more because of the hurt. I'm not so gifted."

"Me either," he said again and blew his hair out of his face. "You better, though. I know you better."

"Yeah? And how do you know?"

He grinned. "You smile."

She made a face. "I smile. That's it?"

"When I first come, you never smile. You have sad always, sad and snappy. Now you smile and do kindness. You better."

"Yeah, well. I have my moments." She chuckled, and he laughed. "Ah, you're not a bad sort, Henri. I just, I'm not..." He put a hand on hers.

"No worries. I know. We friends. Maybe always, maybe more sometime or not, but always we friends. You sleep. I tend fire."

Caden met his gaze, his dark eyes sincere as they shone in the firelight. "Well, wake me up in a few hours. Then you can get some sleep too," she said, patting her legs. She got up and snuggled into the chair. Her mind wandered, sneaking through different glimpses of the future and reminders of the past. Every few moments, her gaze drifted toward Henri. Life was an odd thing that made no sense.

All was quiet when she woke. The house was warm though the fire went out, and Henri slept on the floor. Jolon still snored on the couch with Deb tucked in beside him. Outside, rain still fell though the wind seemed to settle down somewhat. Though her muscles ached, the pain was nothing worse than usual. All seemed good, yet something woke her. She shivered, skin prickling. An acidic stench like the pits of Undercity scented the air. A shuffling, scratching sound came from the other room. Caden kicked Henri in the leg.

"Hey. Hey, Henri. Henri, wake up you lug."

He grunted and shook his head his eyes fluttering open. "Huh? What? Oh, fell asleep. Careless, Henri."

Caden rolled her eyes. "Shh. Something's in here."

His broad face scrunched in confusion. "We here."

"No, you lump, aside from us. Listen."

They fell silent. At first, she heard nothing, but in a moment, the scratching began again. This time a low growl and heavy steps accompanied it.

"Ratdog?" he whispered.

She shook her head. "Too large. Wake Jolon. Quietly." She nudged her little sister. "Hey, girl. Time to get up." Before her sister spoke, Caden put a hand on her lips. "Shh."

Deb was a smart girl and came alert in seconds. Jolon took a little longer, but sat up and rubbed his eyes.

"Something is in the back room," she whispered.

A crash and moaning howl over by the door made everyone freeze, wide awake and terrified.

"Time to go," Caden hissed. She grabbed Deb as Henri uncovered the window.

"It might be nothing," Jolon objected though his voice trembled.

A high-pitched screeching yowl cut through from the other room.

"That's not nothing."

Henri stuck a small table in front of the window and climbed through. Caden assisted as Deb climbed on and jumped into the brute's arms. After he put her down, he caught Caden's hand and supported her through the window.

Halfway through, she stopped and turned back toward her brother. "Come on, Jolon. Hurry."

He sat frozen on the couch, staring toward the back passage. "It's some kind of cat."

Caden leaned in through the window. Sharp green/gold eyes stared at Jolon through the dark. The monster stepped into the partial light, crouching with a snarl on its face. "If that's a cat, it's a bloody huge one. Move Jolon, before you're its supper!"

"Ahh," her brother squealed, hunching up on the back of the seat.

The massive cat sprang and almost caught him as he fell behind the furniture. Caden snatched up a book and threw it at the creature. The angry feline yelped and jumped high, coming down with its claws extended.

"Henri, help," she exclaimed, throwing another book. Poised on the rickety table, she snagged anything near her and kept up the attack "Jolon, move."

The brute let go of her and disappeared. Nor could she tell where her brother was. The room was too dark, and all she saw was the giant cat snarling at her. She swore as she realized she had run out of ammunition. Desperate, she pulled down the remains of a curtain and wrapped a shard of the window.

"Jolon?" she called, watching the animal stalking her. It crouched low, preparing to pounce. She caught movement from the corner of her vision. Jolon; he was inching his way along the floor, making his way to the front door. Distracted, she almost didn't see the monster cat leap, but she moved at the last moment and sliced at it as she fell to the floor. For just a moment, she felt as though she was a glass figurine shattering into pieces. Every part of her body pulsed with pain; her vision hazed over, and she almost blacked out. The animal would get her; she had no doubt.

"Come on," someone shouted and rough hands hauled her from the floor.

She grunted some kind of something, but couldn't seem to move. Icy rain saturated her clothes, causing her to shudder. Coughing, she forced her vision to clear.

"Henri?" she gasped.

He peered down at her, his hair stuck to his stern face. "We go, we go," he said as she realized they were running through the trees.

"The others?" she asked, trying to see where her siblings were.

"They good, they come."

Branches whipped about them as he ran. She gasped as each thump of his feet sent jarring pain through her limbs. "Slow down. Henri, slow."

"Can't," he puffed. "Monster injured. Huge mad. After us," he said, his fragmented words coming between huffing breaths.

She wasn't certain how long they ran on like that. The ground was rough, and Henri stumbled many times, but he didn't stop. She couldn't see where her brother and sister were. All she could do was cling to Henri. Despite herself she cried, grateful raindrops hid her tears. Perhaps it was the pain or the terror, or the chilling water that drenched her, but she had lost her steel, and it made her angry.

"Stop, stop," she shouted, hitting him on the arm.

He stumbled again and grabbed at a paper-white tree to steady himself. Caden swung her legs down, slipping to the soggy ground. Grass and plants clung to her. Deb ran up, and she gathered her sister in her arms, holding her tight.

"Guys, guys, there's another building here."

She turned Jolon's way. He stood leaning against a rusted sign, doubled over and grunting, but he flicked a hand toward a shattered glass door. Caden forced herself to her feet. She grabbed a broken branch and used it to limp to the entrance, pulling Deb with her.

"Wait," Henri said and rushed past her. "I make safe."

She shook her head and exchanged a glance with Jolon. Bedraggled, he shrugged. Caden hobbled into the building, leaving Henri to do whatever it was he felt he needed to do. Too exhausted to care if cats, ratdogs, or some other bizarre creature waiting to eat her, she leaned against a display case. Every part of her soaking body gave up. She slumped to her knees.

"Aghk," Jolon groaned as he came in behind her and Deb. "No more running. I'm not made for this kind of adventure." He stumbled over some boxes and sank down on a bench.

Deb clutched Caden's arm, whimpering. "Home, I just want to go home."

Shaking, Caden brushed the dripping strands from her sister's face. "Yeah, me too," she said softly. She edged them over to a wall, and they curled up together against it.

Henri crashed in, making her jump. He had a hunk of pipe in one hand and a few towels in another. "All is clear. Found these in box. Wrapped in plastic. All good."

He tossed one to Jolon before giving a couple to Deb and Caden. She pulled a green one to her face and dried it off before rubbing at her hair. Deb wrapped her bright blue towel around her head and helped Caden dry hers.

"They're soft," her little sister said, her lower lip quivering.

She dug up a smile for her golden child before leaning her head back, closing her eyes.

"It's a store of sorts," Jolon said, and she peeked over at him. "There might be food."

Henri pointed to a door behind him. "Storage room through that way. Some stuff sealed away. Might be good food."

"Doesn't have to be good," her brother said as he got up and limped toward the door. "Just has to be edible."

"Are we safe here?" Deb asked, her voice small and scared.

Henri shoved a unit of shelves in front of the broken door. "We safe now." He glanced down at them, his concern clear on his face. "I make beds. I make warm."

Caden didn't argue; she just closed her eyes again and let herself sleep.

Chapter 9

Cate swore and slammed another cupboard shut. Nothing. She couldn't find anything to warm them. The blankets and clothes were dust. The pots and pans were in useful condition, but no paper or anything to start a fire. She checked on Teddy. His head rested against the back of his chair, and he shivered visibly. She took her outer shirt off and tore off a sleeve. Next she took a couple of ladles from a drawer.

"All right, bud. Let's stabilize your foot," she said, kneeling in front of him. "We're gonna have a cold night, so we need to get cozy, and I don't want you complaining."

She tore her sleeve into strips and secured the ladles on either side of his ankle. He whimpered and moaned as she handled his foot, his fingers gripping the arms of his seat.

"Hey, you smell that?" he asked as she finished.

Cate stood, pushing her hair from her face and sniffing the air. "What?"

"Smoke."

She sniffed again. Yes, smoke. Somewhere a fire burned. Hopeful, she shoved aside the plastic slats covering one window. Rain and foliage obscured her vision, and the scent of smoke was faint.

"So, where one follows smoke, one finds fire, and we need fire," she said under her breath. She pondered Teddy's condition. Any attempt to move him didn't seem like a good option. Still, flames did not pack up in a box for easy transportation.

"If there's a fire somewhere, someone is tending it, I would think."

Blinking, she registered what he meant—people, other people outside, living and making fires... and living. "You think they're okay?"

"Okay? Okay as in they won't eat us or anything? Can't say. Hopefully. Guess we'll have to go find out."

Exasperated, she flicked her eye upward. "Right. You with your leg all twisted up and the rain trying to drown us, and all. We're gonna go strolling off to who knows where following a whiff of elusive smoke."

Despite his drawn appearance and the shivering cold, he donned a wicked grin. "Better than sitting here."

"Ah, you're impossible," she said with a laugh. "So, we're going to freeze chasing after fire? No. We're better off working out a way to get warm here."

He frowned, his eyes narrowing. "You think I can't do it." His face twisted in a grimace as he pushed himself up from his chair. "See? I'm fine. The splint did the work. Let's go."

"Damn, you're stubborn. What do I do with you?" she said with a disapproving twitch of her head.

"Take me to the fire," he grunted and hobbled toward the door.

Hesitating, she glanced about the place. Water started to pool in the corners. There was no telling if the roof would cave in or not. It certainly wasn't getting any warmer.

"Wait," she said, exasperated. She went to one closet in the back and dug around until she found a box of plastic bags. Pulling some out, she tore holes in one and slipped her head and arms through.

"Not bad," he said. "Brings out the pretty green of your eye."

"Pretty green? Are you attempting to flirt?" She thrust a bag at him. "Here."

He studied the makeshift rain gear before pulling the plastic over his head. "Good idea, the bags. I'm not much of a flirter."

"Oh, come on. I've seen you surrounded by the girls. They're all smiles and giggles." She went around him and nudged the door open, checking if the way was clear.

"Yeah, well. That's them, not me."

"I noticed. The way seems clear. I think the storm got rid of the ratdogs." She put her hand out and let the shower soak her skin. "We didn't melt, so I guess we can venture out again."

He turned his hand toward the door. "Guess we go then."

She snorted and grabbed a stick. "Here. Come on."

As they stepped into the downpour, she pulled his arm around her shoulder, and he leaned against her. "We don't even know which way to go."

"Yeah," he said as they hobbled forward. "At least, the bags are helping."

Cate pushed her hair out of her face. "Sort of. The sooner we're out of this wet, the happier I'll be."

Cautious and wary, she surveyed the area. A long stretch of flat went off to their left. It seemed the best route to take considering Teddy's foot.

"It's such a strange thing to think this was all roads and buildings," Teddy said, a hint of pain in his voice. "I can't help imagining the way life used to be—so many people wandering about at their jobs and lives. This all seems unbelievable, the stuff they made and worked for. Nature takes over in a matter of time and everything is gone." They stumbled over some rubble. "Well, most of it."

"This stuff interests you, doesn't it," she asked, her shoulders aching from his weight.

"Yeah, it does."

"Why?"

He stopped for a moment, catching his breath. "'Cause it beats dwelling on how bad things might get."

She didn't say anything, and they continued in silence for quite a while. The air was getting colder as the night stretched on. Soon they wouldn't be able to tell where they were going.

"Oh hell, this was a bad idea," she muttered, her fingers stiffening. "We should have stayed in the shelter. It's too late to go back now."

"We'll be all right." His words slurred as he stumbled and coughed. "We need to rest for a second."

Cate half-dragged him over to a bench covered in vines. He slumped down, putting his face in his hands.

"Just a second," he said, his voice weak. "One second."

The sky was solid grey and getting darker with each passing moment. There had to be somewhere better to stay. She pulled off her plastic bag and draped it over his head.

"You stay here. I'll search around, try to find somewhere to get out of this."

He grunted. "I'll be right behind you."

"Yeah, course you will," she said and petted his head before heading off.

"Henri?" Caden called as a loud thumping woke her. "What are you doing?"

"Humm? Nothing," he said, sitting up from his slumped vigilance of the fire. He rigged a makeshift firebox out of some metal shelves with a pipe taking the smoke out of a window. They could place stuff on top if they wanted and toss bits of wood or anything burnable through the front.

"So what was the noise?" she asked, sitting up.

He rose and turned about as though listening. "What noise?"

"That," she said as a thumping sound came from outside. She got off the floor and wiped the dust off her pants. "Is it the cat monster?" she whispered, lowering her voice as the sound got louder.

Henri picked up a chunk of shelving and stood beside her. "Something outside."

She made a face at him. "No, and here I thought it was a ghost." She rubbed at one of the filthy windows and peered outside. "Can't see anything." A blurred shadow moved in the rain beyond the steps. "Someone else is out there." They exchanged glances. Someone was outside, someone other than them.

"Upperlords?" Henri asked with a shrug.

"Can't see them doing that. They wouldn't leave their kingdom of safety for anything." She peered through the window again. The figure moved closer. It seemed familiar. She smacked Henri on the arm. "Move the shelf. Let them in."

"Let them in? No. We don't...." he protested, but she grabbed him by the shirt.

"Open the damn door. I think it's Cate."

"Can't be," he said, giving her the expression most people gave when they thought she was being ridiculous.

"Can't be? Open up and don't be so condescending. If I'm wrong, fine. If I'm right, that's better."

The brute blinked at her. "K. I open door, but I be ready," he said, holding his metal weapon high.

"What's going on?" asked Jolon, standing behind them. He rubbed his eyes and yawned. "You two can't let anyone sleep, can you?"

Henri pointed his weapon toward the window. "She say Cate outside."

Jolon yawned again. "Seriously? You were dreaming."

Frustrated, she gritted her teeth. "No. Someone's out there, and I'm sure it's Cate. Check."

Sighing, Henri grasped the shelf with his other hand and pulled it away from the door. Jolon seized a hunk of wood and took a wide stance, his pudgy face grimacing in an attempt to appear fierce. Henri took a deep breath and jumped out the door. They heard a yelp and a scuffle. Caden rushed out the door with Jolon behind her. Henri had his back turned to them as he wrestled with someone. The other person yelped and screeched, kicking at him.

"Cate?" Caden yelled as she darted around Henri to discover who he captured.

Her friend thrashed at him, her hair wild about her face. At the sound of her name, she went still and gasped as she recognized Caden.

"What the hell? What are you doing here?" she asked. She whacked at Henri's arms. "Put me down, you lumping lug!"

Henri released Cate, and she stood, glaring at him. "Go do something useful," she turned her glare at Jolon, "you too. Teddy's a ways down that way. He's got an injured ankle and is drowning in this rain." She shook her hands, spraying water. "Nasty stuff. Used to think it was pretty. Awful stuff."

Stunned and confused, they stared at her, not moving.

"What? How...." Jolon muttered as Henri acted like his brain gave up on him as he tried to figure out why she was there.

Caden nudged Henri with her foot. "Get going. We can find out all the details when you get back. Come on, Cate. There's a fire going and towels to dry off with." She dragged her friend into the shop, leaving the others to get Teddy.

Despite the plastic bag covering her, Cate dripped with rain and a faint blue tinged her lips. Caden dumped her friend in front of the fire and threw her a dry towel. They stared at each other, and she chuckled, knowing they were both wondering how the other ended up where they were. "Get dry and I'll search for some food. After, we can compare stories and decide who's the bigger fool."

All the noise finally woke up Deb, who sat up from her nest of blankets and soft cushions, rubbing her eyes. "Oh, hi," she said, yawning. "Did you come to get us home?"

"Sorry, kid, I'm in my own mess."

Caden left them to each other and went in the back room. The storage area was fairly large with shelves and shelves of boxes, some of which barely held together through the effects of time and rodents. She rummaged through them, finding a few cans of food still in good shape. Another shelf held an assortment of dishes and pots. Most were broken, but some still usable. She took her finds and went back to the others.

"Found some edibles. At least, they seem edible. They aren't bulging or dented, or anything like that. Just gotta get them open, and we could have a decent meal," she said, placing her stuff on a counter. She rooted through the shelves and junk, looking for something to use as an opener.

"Here," Deb said, handing her a can opener. "I've seen Ma use one of these." She thrust out her chin. "Told you I can scrounge."

Caden patted her on the head. "Yeah, you make a good gopher. Why don't you take this pot outside and get us some rain water? If we boil it, we might be safe drinking it. Better idea than dying of thirst, anyway."

Deb grinned and grabbed the pot Caden held out to her. "No problem. Gotta pee anyway."

"Yeah, well, keep an eye out for trouble. Don't go far from the door and if you see anything that might be dangerous get back inside. Got that?"

Her little sister nodded and skipped out the door, whistling.

Caden set to making them something to eat. "That girl never surrenders," she said as she dumped the contents of a can into another pot. She stuck it on the top of Henri's firebox and perched on a stool beside Cate. "She's the reason we're out here. Wandered away when no one was looking. Decided to explore what life was like outside." She emptied another can in the pot and stirred, sniffing the steam. "Seems okay, should be safe to eat."

Cate nodded, her head wrapped in the towel and her eye drooping from the warmth of the fire. Worn through, she shivered in her drenched clothes.

Caden tossed a piece of wood on the fire. "You tend the food. I'll see if I can find you something dry to wear," she said as she got up and handed the spoon to Cate. She went in the back and rummaged around some more, pulling down boxes. Most of them fell apart as they hit the ground, spilling their contents everywhere. Several rats and mice went scurrying for cover, but Caden ignored them. Much of what was there was of little use, however, she did discover a box filled with t-shirts still stored in plastic. Another had knit pants that seemed too tight to be comfortable but were stretchy and useable. Still another contained socks and underwear with funny, colourful characters all over them. She gathered up what she thought was useful and went back.

The guys had just come back and were busy propping a sopping Teddy up near the fire. He was just as blue as Cate and pain twisted his features.

"Here." She tossed the clothes to her friend who took them and wandered off to the back to change. Deb went with her, asking endless questions.

As Caden put her hands to her hips, she frowned at Teddy. "Well, you're just a mess, aren't you?"

"There's no need to sound like Ma," he groaned as he rubbed his head with a towel Jolon gave him.

She knelt and tore away the plastic bag. "You're drier than Cate. These bags were a clever idea."

"Yeah, Cate's."

He winced and rested his head back against the rags Jolon stuffed behind him. She put a hand to his forehead. "You're hot. Cate's done a decent job on your foot, but I'll check if I can find better stuff to bind it with. You did a nasty number on yourself. Hope it was worth it."

"Not really. Didn't find out too much. Nearly got caught. Got chased by Under scum and a horde of ratdogs. Fell outside. Not fun."

"Thanks," she said as Henri handed her a bowl of soup.

"Dug up the bowls in back. Spoons too. He okay?"

"Uh, huh, he will be. He only needs to get warm and rest. Check for some kind of first aid kit or something I can bind up his leg better with, please." He nodded and left.

Jolon helped himself to some soup and sat down beside them. She stirred hers around, staring at the brownish orange chunks.

"You want some, Teddy?" He nodded, so she scooped a spoonful, blowing on the food before feeding him.

"So, the gang's all together again, hey?" Jolon said. He stuck another hunk of wood in the fire. "Ain't this fun? Ma and Pa are probably having fits."

Caden grimaced at the thought. "Yep."

Cate and Deb came back carrying several quilted blankets. "Found them all sealed up in zippered plastic bags. Good as new. Soft too," she said and spread one over Teddy. Her colour seemed better, and the clothes weren't too bad though the shirt hung almost to her knees and had a strange alien on the front. She wrapped herself in a green quilt and took the bowl Jolon offered her. "Strange place, this store. All kinds of stuff though most of it's junky plastic and ugly statues."

"It's a bargain store," Caden told her as she handed Deb some food. "They carried almost anything you can think of and all for five dollars or less. We found a couple in the mall. That's where some of the best goods came from."

"Found this in back," Henri said as he came back and gave her a plastic box with a red cross on the top. "Might help."

"Might just," she said as she opened the box. She took out a roll of stretchy cloth. "This will, anyway."

Teddy yelped as she examined his rain-soaked foot. She pulled off his sock. Patters of purple and blue covered his swollen foot, but no bone protruded from the skin. She had seen worse helping her Ma with the injured and wounded of Undercity.

"Doesn't seem to be too bad," she said as she re-bound it. He winced again as she worked. "Sorry. Ma always said I needed to work on improving my touch."

Deb snuggled under the quilt with Cate. "So, you led everyone on a merry chase, didn't you?"

"Yep," she said with a huge yawn. "But the monster cat was the one who chased us out here."

"Monster cat?"

"Big cat," Henri explained. "All teeth and claws."

"Nearly ate me," Jolon said, shivering.

Cate chuckled. "You were afraid of a cat?"

"Yeah, well, you've never seen a cat so big. Bigger than most dogs," he protested and spread his arms out to show how large the animal was. "It would have scared you too."

"So, what now?" Deb asked.

"We set up some beds and get some sleep," she said. Done in, she pressed the heel of her palm against her eye. "We're all tired. This storm might stop soon enough, and we can make our way home."

"Then what?"

They all stared at Jolon, and he shrugged. "We've been outside, and we didn't die or melt, or anything. We can go outside. I mean, there's the cat and all, but that's no worse than anything else we've faced. This changes everything for everyone. Doesn't it?" He glanced at each of them in turn. "Doesn't it?"

Caden stared at the flames. "I guess."

Chapter 10

Cate huddled in her quilt and stared at the fire. She convinced the others to let her tend the fire while they all slept. Sleep wasn't something she felt would come anytime soon.

They could live outside.

Restless, she scanned the store. The building was a mess, unsafe with broken walls and a weak ceiling. Still, the place held lots of useable stuff. The little apartment with the courtyard had charm, yes, but was still attached to all those others. This was away, open and free, a place where she could breathe and grow things. This was a home she could truly make her own.

Sighing, she sunk back in her blanket and rubbed at her face. Caden curled up with Deb on a pile of mats Henri dug up. Teddy was in a fitful sleep his hair plastered to his brow. His lips moved as he muttered incomprehensible words. She took the remains of her shirt and wiped his forehead. They could visit. The towers couldn't be too far away.

Yeah, he was attractive and cool to be with. A tingle ran through her lips, and she put her fingers to them. The kiss was pleasant too. Still, to arrange her life around him was something she refused to do, especially since she doubted his interest. It was probably all a part of the adventure.

She frowned at him. Pest. Weary, she got up and walked about, stretching as she glanced out the window. The rain stopped, and the moon found its way out from behind the clouds. With a glance back at the others, she eased the shelf away from the door a crack and slipped outside.

A shiver ran through her as she glanced about. The area was so quiet. Drips of leftover rain fell from leaves and branches, making rhythmic pats on the ground.

In Undercity, the constant drone of air systems always accompanied life. The sound was ever-present under the rumble of the people going about their wretched days. Even in the tower silence never lasted long.

Here, though, here, the quiet made her ears hurt.

With her senses on the alert for any animals, she stepped out into what was once a road. Bits of cement still poked through the grass and weeds trying to devour the surface. As she caught her lip between her teeth, she closed her eye and spread her arms out wide, absorbing the vast beauty surrounding her.

No, she would not go back, not for him or anyone.

Restless, she stood alone for quite a while before she went back inside and stoked the fire. By the time Jolon took her place, fatigue ate at her bones. When she woke in the morning, she was still tired. The others were all up and eating more soup. Numb and groggy, she took her share, but barely tasted it.

"What do you think?" Deb asked, twirling. Several layers of bright t-shirts covered her. "Found them in the back all sealed in plastic."

"Strange stuff, plastic," Teddy said, sitting on a folding metal chair with his foot on a box. "Keeps stuff intact that should degrade with time."

"Good for us," Jolon said, slurping soup. "There're plenty of things we wouldn't have if it hadn't been sealed in plastic."

"True, but more plastics are falling apart now. Some day, all the stuff from the past world will disappear."

Cate grinned at Teddy and sat down beside him. "Look at you, spouting knowledge and doom. I would say you're mending."

"I'm doing all right," he said. "Foot still hurts like fire, though, but I'll live. Thanks for everything."

"Don't get too soppy, old guy. I might think you like me." The instant she spoke, she wished she hadn't as Jolon and Deb cackled with laughter and kissing sounds.

Teddy flushed and scowled at them. "Ah, you two check what supplies you can collect in the back."

"Go on," Caden added as they continued to heckle.

They left, chuckling. Caden sat down beside her while Henri crouched by the fire, stirring the ashes with a stick.

"Found lots working lighters," he said, patting the pocket of his grey overcoat.

Caden tugged at a sleeve. "Cute coat. Fits good."

The brute grinned a little. "Found in back hanging on rack. Still good condition."

"Any more back there? Coats?" Teddy asked. He put his empty bowl to the side and leaned forward, careful of his foot.

"A few," Henri shrugged. "Some still good, some not so. Want me get some?"

"Yeah, try and get enough for everyone. Yes, the rain's stopped, but I would rather not get soaked again," he replied, and Henri left with a nod.

"All right, old guy, what are you up to?" Cate asked, watching him with narrowed eyes. Irritated with his incessant ability to take charge in an instant, she bristled. "You're all fine and charging ahead. Not much keeps you down, does it? The hero rises again."

His face twisted with annoyance. "It's better than dwelling on the pain."

A twinge of guilt nibbled at her, but she shoved the emotion away. "I'm not..."

"So, what's the plan?" Caden asked, changing the subject. She glanced toward Cate, who closed her mouth and looked away.

Good. Let him be all superior and infuriating, makes leaving easier. Despite the frustration fuelling her, a nagging sadness made her doubt.

Teddy leaned back again. "Well, we need to find our way back home."

"That's obvious," Cate muttered, but he ignored her.

"Ma and Pa will worry, and we need to tell everyone what we've discovered."

"What have we discovered?" Caden asked, crossing her arms over her chest. "That going outside can soak you to the skin? That there are animals out here that would love to add people to their diet? So far all the shelters we've found are crumbling back to nature."

"Yeah, but we can get out," he replied flatly. "Now, we don't need to stay in the towers. We can live in them, go back, but not seal ourselves away in them. We can grow things outside; harvest more food, more freedom. Who can say? We might even find more people."

"More kids? That would be terrific," Deb said as she came skipping back.

Jolon followed behind with a couple of packs. He thrust one at Cate. "Guess you will need to take one of these."

"What's in it?" she asked, standing up. The stash didn't weigh much, but she didn't want to haul around useless stuff.

"Blankets and some clothes, mostly." Another sack clunked as he dropped it on the floor. "This one's got more cans of food inside. Thought Henri might lug that about. I got some plastic bowls and some bottles in this one," he added and held up a bright orange pack. "I figure we put some of the rainwater we boiled in them to bring."

"Good plan," Teddy said. "Good job." He struggled to get up, and Caden lent him an arm.

"Oh, yeah, found some crutches. Figured you might like them, limpy," Jolon said with a grin. He dropped the other pack and went back to the storage room.

Cate snatched up the stash with the bottles and filled them, deciding to stay at the store. She thought they might complain and protest, at least, Caden would. Didn't matter. She stuffed the full bottles back in the stash and turned back to them.

"Got coats," Henri exclaimed, cutting her off. He tossed one at her.

She caught the navy blue garment and put it on. It wasn't too bad, warm and lined with some kind of soft material.

"Here you go," Jolon said, holding out a pair of crutches to Teddy.

After he put on the black coat Henri gave him, he put the crutches under his arms. "Thanks. At least now I can hobble along with the rest of you."

They all smiled, happy and ready to get on with their adventure. Cate rolled her eye as she slung the stash to her back.

"Yeah, but which way are we going?" she asked as they went outside. The day was cloudy, and everything glistened with wet though the air was warm. She stopped in the road. "That's the way we came. We might be able to get back into the buildings, but there are ratdogs lurking about."

Caden pointed to the left and back. "When we left the bookshop, we went away from the building and found the cat's house."

"The cat might be anywhere," Jolon said.

"Thing is vicious," Henri chipped in. "Might be more of them too."

"Yeah, but if we can go back to the building, we can follow along the outside and, hopefully, find our way back to the bookshop while avoiding the cat."

"So, we've got ratdogs or vicious cats, not much choice," Jolon scoffed. "I vote for the ratdogs. We know how to handle them, or at least, we have a better chance of facing them than a monster cat with who can say how many followers."

"Back that way it is." Teddy pointed one of his crutches to the left.

Cate didn't wait for the others to agree, she strode off at a good pace and set herself apart, getting ready to separate. The habit grew from years of leaving. Teddy's lame leg slowed them down, which allowed her to keep ahead of them.

"What's up?" Caden asked, puffing a little to keep pace as she came up beside her.

Reluctantly, Cate slowed a little. She would never intentionally hurt her friend; it was too much like poking at a baby. "Nothing, just keeping a lookout for any potential hidden dangers," she said, hoping her lie sounded genuine.

"You sure you're not running?"

"Do I look like I'm running?" she answered a little too abruptly. Aggravated, she caught the expression on Caden's face and frowned. "Maybe a little," she admitted. "Actually, this is more like sidestepping than running. You know, making my own path."

"That's an excuse."

"Oh, thanks."

Her friend caught her arm, but Cate kept walking. "Why?"

Frustrated, she blew out a long breath, sending her bangs dancing. "You wouldn't understand. You never have."

"That's no reason not to tell me."

"Hey, you don't like when people push you, why do you think it's okay to push me?" she demanded though knots of guilt twisted her insides.

They walked on for a few moments, Caden staring off in one direction and Cate in the other. The situation was ridiculous. All she needed to do was say she wasn't going back to the towers, but her insides were gooey angry and the words stuck in all the muck.

"You don't want to go back."

Her friend's words smacked into her, and she almost stumbled. It sounded terrible said aloud. She worked her jaw before nodding. "Something like that," she muttered and walked a little faster.

Caden caught up with her. "But what about that place, the room you found?"

She whirled around and stopped. "What place?"

Her friend halted beside her, her gaze stern. "The place with the cats and the courtyard with all the flowers. Yes, we found your apartment. Hey, I understand you don't like being with people much. I've known that forever, but out here isn't the only answer, is it? The other place is pleasant. Why not live there?"

Cate jabbed a finger at her. "You want to know why I want to stay out here? That's why, 'cause people are always finding what's mine. They're always invading what's mine and taking it, or ruining it, spoiling it, so nothing is mine anymore." She twisted away and strode on, trying to ignore her friend as Caden rushed after her. Her eye stung, which meant stupid tears she had no use for.

"That's..., oh dang, you can be so frustrating," Caden spat, and Cate tried to ignore her. "Why do you always run? And that's what this is, running. Don't give me any of this stupid sidestepping garbage. Just because we found your home, doesn't mean we won't respect the place or take anything from you. Hell, I might take up one across the hall, if it's as homey as yours."

"Why? Why would you do that?" she barked, furiously wiping at her eye. "You've got a home and all the mushy caring stuff that goes with it. Your dang parents are probably flipping garbage with worry and trying to find you. Nobody anywhere is trying to find me, buddy. Nobody has even realized I'm gone."

"That's 'cause we're all out here with you, silly," Caden shot back. "Now slow down before you need to carry me."

A stab of guilt caught Cate in the gut. She cut her pace in half though she kept her gaze straight ahead. "Yeah, well..." she stopped, all her thoughts running away from her. Vexed, she ground her teeth together, deciding her best option was to shut up.

By mid-morning, they covered a fair piece of ground. They found a dry mossy spot by a tree and sat down. The sun burned away most of the clouds and everything was shiny and fresh.

Henri pulled out some of the food he stored in his pack. "Rrrice craeers, creekers."

"Crackers." Teddy took one from him. "Not bad."

Confusion covered the man's face. "Which, reading or cracker?"

He chuckled. "Ah, reading, cracker's more like eating paper."

"So, we should be close to home, shouldn't we? Caden asked, taking her share of the food. She pointed at the broken buildings a short distance from them. "If that's where you two escaped, you were pretty close to the tower, yes?"

Cate shrugged and kept her eye on her food.

"Hard to say." His gaze slid toward her. If he suspected something was up, he wasn't saying. "We twisted around so much in the vents, I'm not sure how far we went."

"So what do we do?" she asked.

"Uh, we could climb up there and check if we recognize anything," Jolon suggested, pointing to a high mound of rubble now covered in moss and grass.

"You volunteering?" Teddy asked, and he shrugged.

"I guess."

Cate got up and wiped herself off. "Come on. I'll go with you. Probably not gonna see much more than more green, but it beats sitting around here."

"I'll come too," Caden said, and they all gave her a disapproving frown. "Oh, stuff it, all of you. I'm not going to break climbing a hill. Besides, I feel pretty good today."

"Yeah, but..."

She cut Teddy off. "We've done worse than this scrounging."

Henri shuffled on his feet. "I'll go too."

Caden frowned at him as he offered his arm.

"What? Curious," he insisted.

"Right," she said and started up the rubble. The climb wasn't too bad. Several pieces of brick and rock stuck out of the ground, giving her something to step on. Knee-length grass waved about unharmed by last night's storm. The view from the open hilltop stretched out in an endless vista.

"What are those?" she asked, pointing toward some dome-shaped buildings far in the distance to the right. Sunlight danced off them, making them glitter in the sunlight.

Jolon put a hand up to shield his eyes. "I think those are the greenhouses. At least, that's my guess."

"Greenhouses, as in Uppercity greenhouses?" Cate asked, and Jolon nodded.

"Think so." He pointed behind them. "Which I think means the tower is that building over there. See the one three down after those broken ones?"

"How do you know?" Caden asked, shielding her own eyes as she looked where he pointed. She discerned several piles of rubble with half walls and empty windows. After that stood a building with vines climbing up its sides. "You mean the one that's still in good condition?" Made sense, she decided. The structure appeared to be the only one worth living in.

"Yeah, that's the one. I figure if we head off that way, it will lead us back to the bookstore, I think."

"Why doesn't 'I think' sound good?" Cate asked with her fingers clutching her hair.

"Why do people always doubt me?" Jolon said, but Caden ignored him.

The last thing she wanted to get into was a discussion about her brother's reliability. "Come on. We still have a long way to go, and we don't want to spend another night out here scrounging for a shelter."

By the time they made their way to the building Jolon was certain was their home, the sun was almost down, which made finding their way challenging. They were all so tired they began to stumble on the long grass and roots.

Caden paused and rested against the building. "Wait a second," she said, waving at the others.

Teddy leaned against the building beside her. His face was pale again, and he looked like he wanted to crumple to the ground. Despite this, he chuckled and put a hand on her shoulder. "We're a sad pair, aren't we?"

"We made it, though, I think." She gazed at the building in front of her. "I hope."

"The door should be around here somewhere, shouldn't it?" Jolon asked. He stepped back from the building and glanced about. "That way where the grass is all trampled. See, it's a fairly clear path."

"Nah, ah," Deb said, the only bright-eyed one among them. "This way." She pointed to the far left of where Jolon was pointing. "'Cause I remember this." She patted a fallen tree. "I ventured across it. It was my gangplank like the ones in Teddy's stories. I came from that direction, and the door is over there."

"At least, it's close." Teddy groaned. He got up and hobbled forward on his crutches.

"I need a nap," Caden muttered, following. Somewhere in the back of her exhausted brain, she wondered who made the other path and where it led, but the thought sank away under the weight of fatigue.

Henri followed behind her. She could tell he was ready to catch her if she fell. It was a sweet gesture, so why did it irritate her? He was only being polite. She snuck a peak at Cate who refused to interact with anyone since they started heading back.

Were they both so jaded and scared of intimacy that any sign of kindness made them run?

"And we're home," Jolon exclaimed, opening the door to the back room of the building. "Well, close to home. Only a few more minutes and we're back to hot showers and a good grilling from Ma and Pa." He bowed to each of them as they went through the door.

Cate lingered and scowled as Caden waited to see if she would leave them.

"Fine," her friend snapped with a wave of a hand. "But I'm going back to my place. You bunch can go embrace the happy home."

Teddy went to say something to her, but she rushed past him. "Later, old guy. Enough socializing for now."

Henri patted his back, and they exchanged a glance Caden found suspicious and annoying. Weary, she ignored them for thoughts of her bed. Deb caught her hand, pulling her.

"Come on, I'm hungry and miss Ma. Let's go."

On the way back, Henri ended up carrying Teddy on his back while Jolon lent Caden a shoulder as they went through the stairs and hallways. They paused before entering the sunroom, preparing for the scolding they would face.

"If we put Ted and Cad in front, Ma might get distracted by their condition."

"Yes, let's sacrifice the wounded and weak," Caden drawled. She pushed the door and stepped through. "Come on." Ma and Pa were standing by the gardens with several others. Pa wore his scrounging gear, and they all appeared worried.

Deb skipped around her and raced through the crowd. "Ma, Ma? We're back."

"Child fearless," Henri said as they followed her with reluctance.

"Oh, Deb," Ma said, rushing to her. She scooped up her youngest child and clung to her.

"Don't worry, Ma. We're fine. We went outside, which was amazing except for the storm and the large cat. Those weren't so fun. But we found a shop, and I got some new shirts." She pulled at her t-shirt. "Pretty, right?"

Caden groaned inside as Pa's face went from relief to shock and fear.

"We should have told her not to say anything," Jolon whispered in her ear.

"Didn't think of it. We just wanted to get back," she whispered back.

"Outside," Pa said, his face almost as pale as Teddy's.

"Teddy's injured," Jolon cut in, hoping to change the subject.

Henri put Teddy down, and he sat on the stone edge of one of the garden boxes. Ma went over to him, examining his foot.

"Yeah, uh, I fell," he said, and she scowled at him.

"It doesn't seem to be too bad. Not broken at least. You wrapped it?" she said, glancing up at Caden.

She nodded, avoiding her father's gaze. "Learned from the best."

"Did she say you were outside?"

It was Dorkas, staring at them with narrow eyes. "Outside? As in outside?" He pointed toward the glass ceiling. "Impossible. They lie."

Ma rose and met his gaze with a cold stare. "That's enough for tonight. I don't care where they went. Tonight, they are going to their rooms, having a hot bath and a hot meal, and a good night's sleep. Teddy needs to get off this foot, and Caden's health can't handle this much strain. Good night, Dorkas."

She put her arm around Caden and escorted her away from the crowd. Pa herded the others behind her with Henri carrying Teddy again. Caden was grateful. She was bone-weary. Explanations would wait until morning.

†

Cate woke the next morning determined to tell Caden she was leaving. Teddy was cute, but definitely trouble. She stood out in the courtyard and petted her cat. Yes, her home was wonderful. Well, she could always come back if she couldn't find a better place to live.

She left and ventured to the sunroom. A few people milled about playing with the plants. The day was still quite early, so she figured most of the tower people were at the kitchens. The thought of food made her stomach grumble. She rubbed it. It wouldn't hurt to get a good meal in before leaving.

As she passed the grand fountain, she halted for a moment. A few of the more brutish types lingered around the door to the mall. They huddled together whispering amongst themselves and shifting uneasily.

A shiver ran down her spine. It was the same feeling she got when something bad was about to happen, an instinctive reflex, which kept her from harm many times in the past. Hastening her pace, she left them behind.

"Cate," exclaimed Deb as she entered the eating area. The young girl waved at her excitedly and pointed to an empty chair at her table. "Sit here. We're about to tell Ma and Pa about our adventure."

She took a seat while Ma handed her a plate filled with food. Teddy sat across from her with his foot propped up. He smiled at her, and she shovelled a forkful of potato mash in her mouth. Caden shot her a puzzled expression, but she ignored her too.

"Hey," Jolon greeted with a yawn. "So terrific being back in a real bed. Funny how luxuries are easy to get used to."

Henri straddled the seat across from her, his broad face troubled.

"What's up, big guy?" Teddy asked, nudging his arm. "You look like the world is about to fall apart."

"Huh? Oh, not sure," he replied with a shrug. "Went to post this morning. New guy there. Didn't recognize him. Said I not needed anymore." He glanced over at Caden's Pa. "That true?"

"What? No," their pa answered, his eyebrows drawn together in concern. "The rotation is the same as always. Nobody new."

"Didn't think so," the brute said with a gruff grunt. He grabbed a spoon and filled his mouth full.

"You didn't recognize the new guy?" Teddy asked.

Henri shook his head. "Nope. Ugly, slick and bulky with much hair here." He gestured to his chest. "Shirt undone; all that curling, egh."

Ma placed her clenched hands in front of her. "Doesn't sound familiar at all and I've seen everyone in our community, even those who prefer solitude."

"A bunch of strange looking brute types was hanging around the mall entrance this morning," Cate said before she could stop herself.

Everyone turned toward her, and she cursed herself for speaking. "Didn't recognize them either. Though I don't know many here. They were strange like they didn't belong."

"Did you really go outside?" Georges asked as she joined them. She snagged a chair from another table and sat down beside Teddy.

Cate cast a glance at the former Upperlord. The others had talked about her many times, but this was the first time the woman got in her personal space. Eccentric, that was the word Teddy used to describe her. The swirls of red and blue on her blouse complimented her coal black complexion and golden eyes. As she tossed her bright green tie over her shoulder, she perused the food, poking at a piece of potato.

Teddy nodded and winced as he moved his leg too quickly.

"I led them out," Deb cut in, unaware of the seriousness of her transgression. "We would have come back sooner, but this tremendous crashing storm came up all sudden and almost drowned us. We had to run for cover. The first place we found wasn't too bad until the wildcat showed up. It was huge with giant teeth and eyes and tried to eat Jolon."

"Deb," Caden scolded. "Your sense of the dramatic is getting away with you. It wasn't so bad though we did get soaked."

"And this cat?" Ma asked, her eyes tight with disapproval.

"The animal was big," Jolon insisted, his cheeks tingeing pink, "but we got away. No one was hurt."

She turned toward Teddy. "And you, how did you sprain your ankle?"

He traded a glance with Cate. "I fell. Not far, landed wrong, though," he explained, and she wondered why he didn't want to tell his parents where they went exploring.

She kept silent, though. His reasons were his own, and she had no need to get in the way.

"Lies."

Startled at the venomous voice behind her, Cate twisted around. Dorkas was there with his group of followers. Among them were the men she saw earlier, a nasty looking bunch with an obvious purpose.

"Dorkas," their father began, getting to his feet. "My children don't lie. If they said they went outside and survived, they did."

The snake of a man slithered around to the head of the table. "Yes, you'd like that, wouldn't you? Cause more trouble. Stir things up and make yourselves all important."

"What are you talking about?" their father asked.

Henri went to get up, but Georges put a hand on his arm. "Fantastic little bunch of cohorts you acquired. Don't think I've seen some of them about before."

He scowled at her. "Shut it. You have no power here. You're nothing but a washed up lush."

Henri jumped to his feet, thrusting back, so his chair crashed to the floor. "You bad man."

Two of Dorkas' brutes stepped between him and Henri. Caden stood in front of him, her hands on the man's chest.

"No, he's not worth it," she whispered, and he backed away though he huffed anger so intensely Cate expected smoke to billow out of his ears.

"What are you up to?" Pa asked.

Cate got up slowly so as not to draw attention to herself. Whatever was up, she didn't want to be a part of it. Carefully, she edged away from the table.

Dorkas laughed, a foul sound. "We're putting things back right. You think you could keep this paradise to yourselves? You lot aren't good enough for this place. No. We're here to put things back the way they should be."

Georges got to her feet, leaning over the table toward him. "What do you mean, back right?"

The creep smirked. "You lot, you think that this all about equality and community, but I know different."

"Do you? Please, enlighten us," Georges said with a tight grimace.

"This is about power."

Georges froze at the sound of the voice behind her. She rose and turned as the room fell silent.

"Belinda, wow, long time no miss," she drawled and leaned against the table though her hands shook. She folded her arms in front of her. "Where did you come from?"

A squat woman with a bitter scowl stood in front of Georges. Cate's breath caught in her chest as she recognized Sticks and Wedge by her side.

"We followed your spies," Belinda said and flicked a dismissive wave toward Teddy.

"But we lost you," he said, all colour draining from his face.

"Ha, ha," cackled Sticks, though his laugh ended in a cough and he collapsed against Wedge, who had his arm wrapped in bandages. "Maybe. Maybe you just led us to finding your hiding place."

"Yeah, you thought you were clever. Not so clever now, eh?" Wedge said and dropped their packs on the table.

"Quiet!"

"Yes, Upperlord," both Sticks and Wedge said, bowing.

Cate stared like everyone else around her. The squat, bitter woman took on a superior twist to her stern face. Behind her was a wall of brutes, each of them holding some kind of pipe with a handle. She guessed it was a weapon, but didn't understand the mechanics of it.

"Oh, crap," swore Jolon, and she jumped, not realizing he was beside her.

"What?" she hissed.

"Those things they're holding, they're guns."

"Guns?"

"Ah, huh, they put holes in things and people from a distance. Don't know where they got them. Every time we found weapons like that, Pa threw them into the sludge pit."

"Oh, hell. We led them here," she whispered, pulling him further away from the table.

"That's Georges' sister. She's a mean piece of scum and, yes, she's an Upperlord. Turns out Dorkas works for her. Big surprise."

Their father stepped forward, holding out a hand. "Welcome, Belinda. There's plenty of room..."

The Upperlord cut him off. "Don't be disgusting. You think you could hide something like this from Uppercity?"

"We never meant to...."

"Yes, you did," she said, scanning the room. She threw a dismissive wave toward Dorkas. "You, go help secure the rest of these... usurpers."

"Ah, Belinda, always the rat," Georges said, stepping between Jolon's father and her sister. "And now you gnawed your way here. What do you want?"

The Upperlord paced. "Want? I want nothing. Thanks to you and your friends, I now possess everything I could want."

Georges chuckled. "And why do you think you can slither in here and take over?"

"Slither? First a rat now a snake, that is no way to talk to your sister," she snarled, stopping in front of Georges.

"You're a slithering rat-snake, Lindy."

Belinda shook her head. "You possess no family loyalty. You never have. You've been useless since we were children, and deceitful even now." She pulled out a small version of one of those gun things and pointed it at her sister.

Georges laughed. "Those things don't work. You never found bullets. So, unless you plan on hitting me with it, it won't help you much."

Her sister pointed the gun toward the ceiling. An ear-shattering explosion sent people screaming and cowering toward the floor.

Jolon's father stepped forward once more. "This isn't necessary, please."

"You," Belinda snarled. "You always thought yourself above your proper place. I should have gotten rid of you years ago, but you had your uses. Did you honestly think I wasn't watching you?"

"Why, Belinda...."

"Upperlord Belinda, Undercity scum."

"Upperlord, this doesn't need to...."

"Quiet, I have no interest in you anymore." Her gaze slid to Deb and Teddy. "Your children, however, have their uses."

"That's enough, Belinda," Georges said, stepping toward her sister. She reached for the gun, but the Upperlord pulled away. Jolon's father tried to intervene, and they struggled. The whole

Peterson family screamed as the gun went off again. Panic coursed through the room; people scattered.

"Stop them!" ordered Belinda, waving her gun toward the crowd.

Terrified, people shoved and scrambled to get away. Cate grabbed Jolon and pulled him toward the back hall. Shock covered his face.

"Come on," she said. "We can't help here." She dragged him through the back halls, working her way to somewhere safe.

Jolon followed numbly as though moving in his sleep. They came to the end of a hall and went through a door to a stairwell. She didn't stop but pulled him downward. They stumbled down the steps until she found an open door. Drained and panting, she hauled him through. He collapsed on the ground and threw up. The place grew dim as the door closed. She slid down the door and sat on the chilly cement floor. A sliver of a glow came from a lamp someone left burning low on a hook on a nearby pillar.

Someone was here. Was this the way the Upperlord entered? No, they showed up in the mall. This was a parkade on the opposite side from Uppercity. No, this was someone else.

The sound of footsteps resonated through the door. She scrambled away.

"Jolon, Jolon, come on. They're coming," she urged, pulling at his shirt.

"No, no, I can't," he gasped. "My Pa."

She hauled him to his feet. "We need to go. Your pa is probably fine. We didn't see anything clearly, and we can't help anyone if we get caught."

He stumbled but followed her. "You truly think he's okay?" he pleaded, snuffling.

"Sure," she said, hiding her doubts. "Look, someone's living down here, and we don't know whose side they're on. We can't go back, but who can say what's in front of us. I need your help to get somewhere safe."

Jolon coughed and nodded.

"Good, let's go."

"Go where?"

"Wherever we can," she answered and took down the lamp. They headed through the parkade and into the dark.

Main Cast of Undercity: Outside In

Teddy – Second oldest child of Peterson family
    Eyes – brown
    Hair – chestnut
    Complexion – Khaki
    Build – slight

Caden – Oldest child of Peterson family
    Eyes – amber
    Hair – black twists
    Complexion – sepia brown
    Build – tall, boney

Jolon – Middle child of Peterson family
    Eyes – mud brown
    Hair – curly black
    Complexion – copper
    Build – thick

Deb - youngest child of Peterson family
    Eyes – pale blue
    Hair – light blond
    Complexion – ivory
    Build – slight
    Cate – Friend of Caden

Eye - grey-blue
Hair – Rusty Red
Complexion – pale
Build –short, slender
Mr. Truman Peterson
Eyes – pale blue
Hair – black and grey
Complexion – drywall grey
Build – boney

Mrs. Tisha Peterson
Eyes – grey
Hair – frizzy blonde
Complexion – drywall grey
Build – tall

Henri – brute for Peterson family
Eyes – forest green
Hair – thin / dusky brown
Complexion – freckled white
Build – slight

Georges – Upperlord and brute Merchant
Eyes – gold
Hair – long black and grey braids
Complexion – coal black
Build – wiry

Belinda – Upperlord and brute Merchant

Eyes – gold
Hair – black braids and twists
Complexion – coal black
Build – full-figured

Mrs. Fish – Friend of Peterson family
Eyes – gold
Hair – mahogany
Complexion – tawny
Build – tall / physically fit

Mr. Fish – Friend of Peterson family
Eyes – brown
Hair – black
Complexion – copper with beard
Build – brawny

Dorkas – Fellow Underling
Eyes – grey
Hair – grey
Complexion – grey
Build – narrow

Nuna – tower resident
Eyes – brown
Hair – chestnut
Complexion – rusty
Build – solid

Coming Soon!

Keep reading for a preview of
book 3 of the Undercity Trilogy

Inside Out

Chapter 1

Cate rushed ahead of Jolon. It was dark and smelly, the kind of stench that made breathing difficult because the throat and lungs protested the invasion of harmful chemicals. And the dark? Well, the dark was worse.

"I never liked the dark. I hated it before, but since our little trip into sunshine, it just, well, it's darker. I feel like I'm going to dissolve into it and never exist again."

Jolon's rambling wasn't what she wanted to listen to, but it was better than giving attention to the thoughts in her head. Long strands of hair fell across her eye as she whipped her head about, trying to determine where to go next. Frustrated, she swept the rogue locks back and pulled her shirt close over her tank top, the chill of the air cutting through the thin fabric. Images of the outdoors kept invading her brain, and she developed a new, aching yearning for freedom from buildings.

Distracted, she led them forward at a brisk pace though every tunnel looked the same and seemed to go nowhere. "What was that?" she asked, realizing he was still talking.

"Perfect, love talking with you too. You realized I don't know anything about you except you're Caden's friend; Teddy thinks you're almost as interesting as a book, and me? I could easily have left you with the cats."

"So charming. I could have easily left you in the kitchens."

"Hey, I didn't ask you to drag me along." He tugged at her coat. "Drop the pace a little, hey? My one leg keeps up fine, but this other one isn't so peppy."

She frowned at him but slowed. Sweat trickled down his wide nose while his round cheeks puffed in and out from heavy breathing. "Of all the people to get stuck with..."

"I end up with you," he finished for her, returning the disapproving scowl. "Yeah, neither of us likes this or each other, big surprise."

"Well, as long as we both agree, we'll do just fine." As she paused, she passed over the lantern. "Where are we?" she asked as she took out a length of string from her pocket and tied her curls of red hair back.

"Don't know," he said, glancing about, his copper complexion pallid.

"I thought you Petersons knew all about this place."

"Right. I've got the whole area all mapped out in my head. I'm one of those computer thingies Teddy's always babbling about. Pa's the one who explored this area: him and Teddy. I've never been here." He stopped in his tracks and slid down the wall, sitting with his knees drawn up close. "I just need a break. There's a fist in my chest, and it's making a squishy toy out of my heart," he said, his voice just above a whisper. The lantern clanged on the cement as he dropped the light aside before burying his head in his arms. "Tired."

"Ah, you're always tired," she said with a little compassion. She dropped down beside him and huddled close. "Cold in here. We need to find some place better soon."

Jolon sniffed and glanced down both sides of the narrow, empty hall. "Don't think anyone's following us. Maybe we could go back and sneak a peek, see if everything's settled down?"

She shook her head. "Not likely. Those Uppers who showed up are a devil lot, and I think they've taken over your tower world."

"Then we should go back and help."

"How?"

Open-mouthed, he stared as though hoping a brilliant idea would tumble out, but nothing came. "Hate this," he muttered and clenched his jaw shut.

Sore and adrift, she gave him an awkward pat on the arm. "I'm sure everyone is okay. At least, I think so."

"You're terrible at this comforting stuff, you realize that, right?"

"Pththt," she replied, sticking out her tongue. "I'm doing my best. What where those things they had?"

He snatched up a pebble and tossed it against the wall across from them. The stone clacked and clattered as it bounced, the sound echoing down the corridor. "Pa says they're called guns. We always had to keep an eye out for them."

"Find any?"

"Once. Didn't get to keep it or try it out. Pa took it and threw it in the southern pit. He said if our world ever got a hold of guns, life would get much more deadly."

"Too bad he wasn't the only one who thought getting rid of them was a good idea."

"What are you doing here, Jolon?"

Startled, they scrambled to their feet. Cate snatched up the lantern and held it in front of her ready to use it as a weapon if she had to.

The woman standing before them was older than Caden's parents, but well groomed with several braids of grey hair wrapped around her head, a rusty, freckled complexion, and eyes the colour of polished wood. She was fairly thick and wore several layers of shirts over a heavy floral skirt.

"It's okay." Jolon placed a hand on her arm. "It's Nuna, the one who found the tower first."

With a hesitant step, he hugged her, his expression revealing his relief.

"Woah, well, what's this? What's going on, boy?" she asked, pushing him away to see his face. "You and your girlfriend get lost?"

Cate put up her hands, the light flickering around them as it swung. "Oh, wait. He's not, I'm not...."

"No, we're not anything or lost. Well, yeah, sort of... lost that is. Not the other thing. Teddy's the one... ugh," he grunted as Cate caught him with her elbow.

Nuna chuckled and beckoned them to follow. "Come on. Let's get you back to where you belong. It's cold down here if you're not dressed in layers."

"No, we can't go back," both he and Cate said.

"Huh? Why?"

Cate exchanged a glance with Jolon, unsure of where to start.

Sighing, Nuna wrapped an arm around Jolon. "Come on, back to my place. First, we'll warm you both up and sort out what's what after that."

"Don't you need a light?" Cate asked as they went.

"Nope. Not in these parts," she said with a touch of pride. "Know them too well. Besides, I got electric lights running just a couple of turns from here."

Jolon shuddered and kept beside her, taking comfort in the older woman's presence.

Cate dropped back behind them, overwhelmed by recalled impressions of the attack of the Upperlords. Every step they took reverberated through the passageway like the horrible explosion from Belinda's gun, making her breath catch in her chest. The screams, chaos, and memory of Jolon's father falling to the ground—she wanted to forget, but couldn't.

People, why did she ever get involved with people? They were unreasonable and untrustworthy and had issues she didn't understand.

The Adventure Continues in Book 3
Coming January, 2016
Get your copy at
www.krismoger.com/books

Like this book? Please, leave a review.

Your kind words are greatly appreciated. Reviews are an author's lifeblood. They are what keep us warm in the winter and fed in the summer. Every review helps readers find this book and others on Amazon. Plus, after months of writing and editing, a good review keeps an author writing. So, please leave a review on Amazon. Thank you.

Juliette Studios Free Giveaway

Get **Mischief and Magic**, a collection of short stories and Undercity extras, **Free!**
Plus, keep up with all new releases, contests, giveaways, and other extras.

Sign up for our newsletter at <u>www.krismoger.com</u> and get your own ebook copy of Mischief and Magic.

Connect with us at -
Facebook: www.facebook.com/juliettestudios
Twitter: www.twitter.com/juliettestudios
Instagram: www.instagram.com/juliettestudios

Author Page

Kris Moger - The Words and Ideas

Like many creative people, Kris Moger doesn't like writing bios, but she got talked into it this time. On an average day, she likes to write, draw, and daydream. On most days, she cleans house, gets distracted, and procrastinates. She has been creating stories since she was young, but only started writing them down in the last dozen years. After publishing a couple of short stories, and corresponding with publishing companies and indie authors, Undercity 1 is her first official published novel.

Proof

Made in the USA
Charleston, SC
13 January 2016